"I'll make you a bet."

"A bet?" Mike leaned forward.

"I bet you that I'll have a front-page story printed before you will." Tess was going to get a story so hot it would burn his feet.

A sly grin lit his face. "Tell you what. Whoever wins cooks the loser dinner."

She had a bad feeling about this. "And what does the loser have to eat?"

"Crow. That's the bet. Take it or leave it."

"Oh, I'll take it. I'm not afraid of you."

Mike put his hand on the doorknob, then suddenly turned. "Maybe you should be." He pulled her into his arms.

With a moan, Tess gave in to it, in to him, welcoming the onslaught of emotions as his tongue plunged inside her mouth. She met him need for need, tangled in the warmth and strength of him.

When he broke the kiss, she stared at him with blank shock, his own surprise mirrored back.

"Oh, my," she said. "This could complicate things."

"Count on it."

Dear Reader,

I love movies. My favorites are still the old black-and-white romantic comedies. *It Happened One Night*, *His Girl Friday* and *Roman Holiday* are just three that spring to mind where the hero is a newspaper reporter.

I'm a former newspaper reporter myself and I still have fond memories of those deadline-crazy days. I thought it would be fun to write my own romantic comedy about a pair of competitive newspaper reporters after the same big story. And I was right. It was fun.

Tess Elliot and Mike Grundel are mismatched lovers from the opposite ends of the social spectrum, but they share a love of the movies and a keen nose for news. This is the first of three books, all written about the same two rival newspapers in the fictional town of Pasqualie, Washington. Watch for the sequels, *A Hickey for Harriet* and *A Cradle for Caroline*, in Harlequin Duets in April 2003.

It always makes my day when I hear from a reader. You can drop me a line at Nancy Warren, P.O. Box 37035, North Vancouver, B.C. V7N 4M0, Canada. Or come visit me online at www.nancywarren.net.

Happy reading,

Nancy Warren

Books by Nancy Warren

HARLEQUIN TEMPTATION
838—FLASHBACK

HARLEQUIN BLAZE
19—LIVE A LITTLE!
47—WHISPER
57—BREATHLESS

HARLEQUIN DUETS
78—SHOTGUN NANNY

HOT OFF THE PRESS
Nancy Warren

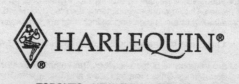

HARLEQUIN®

TORONTO • NEW YORK • LONDON
AMSTERDAM • PARIS • SYDNEY • HAMBURG
STOCKHOLM • ATHENS • TOKYO • MILAN • MADRID
PRAGUE • WARSAW • BUDAPEST • AUCKLAND

This one's for Susan Lyons,
a fellow writer and a good friend.
With thanks.

ISBN 0-373-69115-7

HOT OFF THE PRESS

Copyright © 2003 by Nancy Warren.

Visit us at www.eHarlequin.com

Printed in U.S.A.

1

Excerpt from "Screen Notes" by Tess Elliot, *The Pasqualie Standard*, February 10:

Two new movies opened this weekend: A Country Wedding *and* Boneblaster III. A Country Wedding *is an intelligent, warm and visually entrancing film based on the nineteenth century novel. I highly recommend this sensitive portrayal of a woman caught between the restrictions of the class system and the desires of her heart.*

If you prefer to watch steroid-enhanced, testoster-one-pumped lunks chase silicone-puffed bimbos while blowing up a lot of stuff, you'll love Boneblaster III.

Excerpt from "Mike's Movie Picks" by Mike Grundel, *The Pasqualie Star*, February 10:

Boneblaster *fans, the movie we've been waiting for blasted onto local screens this week, and wow! BBIII is the best yet. Hans Grosskopf annihilates outer space commandoes with awesome artillery, saving the world and bedding babes in black leather. When he stands over the smoking ruins of his warrior foes and says, "You had it coming, scumbags," you can feel that line going down in movie history. BBIII gets a big high-five from Mikey.*

Also new this weekend a real groaner of a snooze-fest,
A Country Wedding. *A bunch of snotty English
folks spend three days getting married. I mean, come
on. Nobody heard of a Reno quickie over there? A Co-*
matose Wedding *gets this week's Rotten Tomato.
Until next week: "You had it coming, scumbags!"*

MIKE GRUNDEL sauntered into the movie theatre and
the smell of popcorn hit him like a left hook to the gut.

Lunch had been an apple and a Babe Ruth bar on
the fly while he'd tried to nail down a source—a
source who didn't want to be nailed—on the Cadman
story. Dinner—well, that would be popcorn. His
stomach grumbled like a nagging mother reminding
him he wasn't eating properly as he joined the concession line.

In front of him stood a hottie in snug jeans. He tried
to take his mind off his growling hunger by admiring
her splendidly rounded rear and long legs. He smiled
to himself, some of his frustration evaporating as he
edged nearer. He'd know that body anywhere.

Almost touching her elegant back, he eased close
enough to distinguish the subtle color variations in the
strands of her shoulder-length hair: gold, wheat, hints
of platinum. Close enough to smell the citrusy aroma
of her shampoo. She never smelled of perfume—he
assumed she didn't use the stuff. Fine by him. He preferred the scent of woman.

As always, he resisted the urge to touch that glorious hair, though he indulged himself in one last whiff
of citrus that overlaid the pungent smell of popping
corn like a silk veil over gaudy fabric.

"Hey, babe," he said. "Come here often?"

Tess Elliot turned, her hair swinging, giving him another tantalizing hint of lemon. Gentle humor sparkled from clear gray eyes. "Don't you have any original lines?"

He shrugged, deliberately cocky. "Don't usually need them."

She choked on a laugh. "I'm amazed you can stagger around with an ego that size."

"You keep it trimmed," he told her, more truthfully than she could possibly realize. Or maybe she saw more than he'd intended for her gaze widened and the zing of attraction they both persistently ignored crackled through the air.

"I wasn't sure you'd be here tonight," she said softly.

"If it's a new movie, and it's opening in Pasqualie, I'll be here," he said, wishing it weren't the truth. Getting demoted from hard news to movie reviews had been a slap in the face that he'd taken for his own reasons. Still, it rankled.

Amusement flickered across her face. "I may be going out on a limb here, but I predict you'll hate tonight's film. It's a chick flick. Nothing gets blown up."

He moved deliberately nearer, chasing the amusement from her expression and turning it to wariness. At this range he saw that the pearly perfection of her skin had nothing to do with cosmetics. "The kisses will be blown up," he all but whispered, then watched, with his own lazy amusement, as a tinge of pink bloomed in her cheeks.

As always when he and Tess were together, the heat between them ran just below the surface. He toyed with it as a kid might toy with a kite string, pulling it closer, letting it out, but never reeling it all the way in. That would spoil the game.

Or would it? What would the very proper daughter of the very rich and important Walt Elliot do if a recently demoted reporter from a no-account family took it into his head to follow his instincts and kiss her?

Intriguing thought. So intriguing, Mike dropped his gaze to her plump pink lips, almost shockingly sensual in the patrician face. He wondered what her father would do if he found a guy from the wrong side of the tracks making time with his daughter. Mike pictured his cojones hanging from the rearview mirror of Walt Elliot's fancy car like a rich man's fuzzy dice and jerked his gaze back up.

No, thank you. The heat between him and Tess was simply the result of seeing a lot of each other. As soon as he got his real job back, he'd forget all about Tess and her big gray eyes, kiss-me-baby lips and body that begged to be explored.

They'd been staring at each other for a moment too long. Another second and he'd lose what little sense of self-preservation he had left. He'd drag her to him and kiss the breath out of her. Forget her powerful father, forget pulling the tatters of his career back together, forget everything but the feel of her hair running through his fingers, her scent surrounding him and the taste of her on his lips.

"Next?" snarled the impatient teen manning the concession.

Tess blinked and turned to the counter.

Mike released the breath he didn't remember holding. It was as though he'd let the kite out, but the string still stretched, taut with tension. What he ought to do was pull out a machete and cut Tess Elliot loose, out of his dreams. It was only because he was between women that he thought about her so much. As soon as he bagged Cadman, he'd get back in the game and Tess would fade into insignificance.

Her voice was as cool and softly musical as an alpine stream as she gave her order. "Club soda, please."

Club soda, he thought with a mild stab of irritation. He could have guessed. No greasy popcorn for Tess Elliot, no sugary cola. Didn't she ever get her hands messy or her diet unbalanced? "Most people think a movie without popcorn is like sex without an orgasm," he told her as she collected her colorless, calorie-less drink.

She turned and gazed at him with faintly raised brows, princess to peasant. "Rather like attempting an intelligent conversation with you." Drink in hand, she turned toward the theater.

She rarely let him get away with anything, which naturally drove him crazy. How could he help himself wanting her? She was smart, gorgeous, sexy and had a mouth on her that constantly challenged him. He watched her go, her back finishing-school straight, top-to-toe class.

Then it was his turn with the snarly teen. Except the girl simpered when she saw him, light dancing off her tongue stud. A woman like Tess would crush him beneath her Prada heel, but to a teen with a tongue stud and acne, he was hot stuff. *Great.* "Jumbo popcorn, please, extra butter," he said loudly enough for Tess to hear. "And a large cola, extra calories."

If it wasn't bad enough he'd been demoted—condemned—to write movie reviews, insult had been heaped on insult when he discovered the rival paper's reviewer was a dewy-eyed debutante whose daddy had bought her a job.

Mike probably wouldn't have minded so much if she was homely. A hundred extra pounds or so and maybe a bushy moustache or a few well-placed zits and he might have gone easy on her. But damn if the cub reporter didn't remind him of Grace Kelly—and one of the secrets no one, but no one, knew about Mike Grundel was this thing he had for Grace Kelly.

She was cool, sophisticated, unapproachable, but hints of fire glinted beneath the icy surface.

Tess had that quality, only she was more uncertain with it. The Ice Princess in training to be the Ice Queen. The first time he'd seen her he'd almost swallowed his tongue. He'd imagined thawing the ice until she was melting with heat—right under him.

It wasn't going to happen, but that didn't mean he couldn't play mental footsie. What was the harm in that? He slipped into the darkened theater and noticed her about halfway down, perched on an aisle seat. She had a notebook already open and a pen poised above it.

She was so green, he grinned. Who brought a notebook to the movies? Somewhere on his desk he had a press package with all the names spelled properly and glossy stills from the film. As if he'd ever use them. There was even a plot summary in case he fell asleep.

The seat across the aisle from Tess was vacant. He plopped into it, scattering popcorn.

She'd noticed him. He could tell by the way she stared at the blank screen as though all thirteen episodes of *The Jewel in the Crown* were being broadcast simultaneously.

As did many cities, Pasqualie, Washington, had two daily newspapers. The *Standard* was a broadsheet; big on commentary and in-depth analysis, it liked to think of itself as the serious paper. Even Tess's movie reviews featured analysis and pseudointellectual commentary.

But his paper, the *Star*, was a tabloid—the common man's rag. From the scantily clad Star Gal on page three to the big coverage on single moms, union grievances and local crime, the *Star* stayed true to its readers. *Star* stories were short, punchy and dramatic. So were Mike's reviews. He pretty much could have written this one without bothering to darken the theater door, but he had his professional pride. Besides, Tess was here.

Her pen started to tap the blank paper on her knee. Was she analyzing the movie already, before it even started?

What was tonight's flick called again? Something about Paris. Mike leaned in her direction. He assumed a falsetto. "*A Day in Paris* is a simply delightful romantic comedy. Poor little Monique has lost her dog Fifi's diamond collar from Cartier. Luckily, Prince Christian Dior will fight the evil Pierre Balmain for the collar and win Monique's heart, thus showing the eternal struggle of woman to pick the right designer."

Tess gazed at him for a moment, then she leaned across the aisle toward him, close enough that he smelled the citrus scent of whatever she used on her hair. Her lips were glossy as though she'd just licked them, and they parted slightly as she closed the distance between them, her eyes fluttering to half-mast in the classic kiss-me pose.

Mike felt his own eyes widen, his blood begin to

pound and he nearly choked on his popcorn. If reciting a few designer names made her kiss him, maybe he could lure her into his bed with a Tiffany's catalog. Did Tiffany have a catalog? he wondered fuzzily as he leaned forward to meet her halfway.

But she didn't kiss him. Instead she spoke, her nasal drawl sounding like Rocky after a few too many rounds. "Dis here movie, *We'll Always Have Paris*, is nothin' but crap. I'm tellin' yez. What do they want wit' Paris? There's nothin but foreigners there. Save yer money. Wait till *Debbie Does Paris*."

She smiled sweetly. Straightened and turned back to the blank screen.

TESS WISHED Mike would leave her alone so she could get over her embarrassing crush in peace. But not as much as she wished he'd spirit her away on the back of his Harley and do all the things to her she'd fantasized about.

He was her secret ideal man. A heart-thumpingly sexy, motorcycle-riding bad boy with a brain. He was so different from most of the men she knew. In her world, men rode in limousines and most of their brains had been bred out of them.

As she watched furtively, Mike tipped his head back against the seat, presumably for a prefilm doze. As his shoulder-length black hair swung behind him, she caught the glint of a silver earring. She wondered what it would feel like to run her hands through his hair, if the strands were silky to the touch.

She jerked her attention back to the screen while she reminded herself of the obvious: Mike Grundel might be gorgeous, and the kind of fearless investigative journalist she admired, but he insulted her in the deepest way it was possible for anyone to insult her. He didn't take her seriously. He might tease and flirt with her, but he clearly thought she was a little rich girl toying with a job until she married a stuffed shirt with a hyphenated last name.

How dare he look down on her? He was hardly in a position of superiority, professionally or personally. He was suffering from a major career setback after a recent bit of investigative reporting had been a little too fearless. After a blistering attack on local developer and philanthropist Ty Cadman, Grundel's only quoted source claimed to have been misquoted and the *Star*, famous for never, ever apologizing, was forced to print an apology on the front page.

Instead of being fired, as everyone in the news community had assumed, Mike Grundel had been demoted to covering the movies and writing innocuous features. At first she'd read his reviews eagerly, wondering where he and she would agree on films and where they'd differ. It didn't take her long to realize they agreed on nothing. It had become almost humorous, and over the months his reviews had become more outrageously guy-centered, and she'd begun to slant her reviews to her readership. She hadn't meant to, it just happened.

The movie was about to start so Tess put Mike—and her wobbly efforts at unbiased movie reviewing—out of her mind and gave her full attention to the screen. Not even journalism school cynicism and six months of reviewing every foot of celluloid that made it to Pasqualie had dampened Tess's love affair with the screen.

Maybe that's what had made Mike Grundel so attractive to her initially. He'd reminded her of Rhett

Butler, with blue eyes that dared the devil, a grin that could charm a rattlesnake and a bullheaded determination to get what he wanted, whatever the cost. In this case, the cost had included his reputation.

He appeared to be taking his demotion on the chin. He'd taken his movie reviewing gig and turned it into a platform for beer-guzzling macho men everywhere. He took gleeful delight in his chauvinistic reviews. And, she had to admit, she'd begun to counter his attacks with her own brand of feminism. She wondered if he flipped to her reviews the second he got his copy of the *Standard* as eagerly as she turned to his when the *Star* arrived.

Of course, she'd be boiled in oil before she admitted she ever read his stuff.

We'll Always Have Paris was her favorite kind of film. Glamorous actors, glamorous clothes, glamorous Paris. After a few moments she forgot about Mike Grundel snoozing across the aisle and lost herself in the story of unlikely lovers, mistaken identities and a stolen Rembrandt.

She was completely caught up in the movie, giggling helplessly at times, when she noticed a rich chuckle coming from opposite her seat. It couldn't be. But sure enough a quick glance confirmed that Mike Grundel, *Boneblaster* fan, was enjoying a romantic comedy.

He caught her gaze on him and suddenly stowed the grin and made a production of a fake coughing fit. Ha.

When she rose after the movie, so did Mike. He indicated she should precede him up the carpeted aisle, then fell into step when they reached the lobby.

"Enjoy the flick, princess?"

In spite of the fact that she persistently ignored his nickname for her, he just as persistently used it. "Yes, I did. And you?"

He shrugged. "Chick flick."

"Probably that nasty cough of yours drowned out all the best lines," she said sweetly. "You should really get that seen to."

He opened his mouth to retort, but didn't get the chance.

"Aren't you Mike Grundel?" a breathless teenage voice asked from behind her.

Poor Mike. He flashed Tess a helpless glance, but she waved cheerily and kept walking. This wasn't the first time he'd been approached since he'd started reviewing. His picture ran with his byline, so he was a lot more recognizable than she, and, in spite of his outrageously sexist reviews, he certainly had a way of attracting women.

She rather thought his dark good looks with an edge of danger just below the surface, drew women more than his Neanderthal opinions did. She'd laugh if she didn't count her own foolish self as one of the victims of his careless charm.

She didn't turn around, but kept walking toward the adjacent parking lot, the girl's eager questions and Mike's much less eager answers fading as she strode away.

When she got to her car, all thoughts of movies, men and unrequited lust fled her mind. Her red BMW wasn't sitting right. It didn't take much investigation to reveal a flat tire. It wasn't just flat—the tire was shriveled and flaccid, surrounded by chunks of amber glass.

She swore under her breath. She didn't much relish

changing a tire in a cold parking lot in the middle of February, but, if she was quick about it, she wouldn't freeze.

Her father believed a woman with a car should know the basics, and when she was sixteen and got her first compact as a birthday present, he'd taught her himself the rudiments of safety and maintenance.

Disarming the theft prevention device, she unlocked the trunk...and groaned. She was already riding on her spare. The garage mechanic had told her she needed a new tire after the last one punctured, and she'd been saving up from her meager salary. She felt like kicking a wheel, but with her luck she'd ruin yet another tire.

She dragged her cell phone out of her bag and stared at it. Who was she going to call at—she glanced at her watch—nine-thirty at night? Her father? He'd give her a lecture about carelessness then make a big production of taking care of the entire business himself and buying her a new tire. Probably a whole new set. She shuddered. Definitely not her father.

The garage wouldn't have anybody on this time of night. She'd have to take a cab home and sort it out in the morning.

"If you ever want anyone to go with you to the movies, you know, like, uh, for a second opinion or anything...uh...call me."

Tess turned and watched the teenager slip Mike a scrap of paper.

He took it, saying, "I don't—"

But in a cloud of bobbing black hair the giggling girl was gone.

If Tess hadn't been frustrated by her own predicament, she would have laughed at the expression on Mike's face when he caught her watching him.

"Don't lose that number. She's the perfect age for you."

With a scowl he scrunched the paper and tossed it in a nearby trash bin. "Hope I didn't keep you waiting," he said, puzzlement in his tone.

"You didn't." She smiled as if she didn't have a care in the world and standing in the middle of a freezing parking lot was her idea of recreation. She hit the off button on her cell. If he'd just hop on his motorbike and be on his way she could be on hers.

But Mike Grundel never did what she wanted him to do.

"Calling the chauffeur?" His gaze wandered over the sporty red BMW.

As sweet as it was of her parents to buy her the car for a college grad present, she really wished they hadn't. She felt conspicuous driving a pricey import when all the other reporters she knew drove modest vehicles, even derelict beaters. Or, in Mike's case, a sleek black motorcycle. But how could she refuse their generosity? They'd be so hurt.

"Yes," she answered his question semitruthfully. A cab driver was a chauffeur of sorts, after all. "And it's a private call."

He snorted. "See ya."

With a sigh of relief, she watched him walk on. He was passing her car when a tinkling sound had him glancing down to where his booted foot had kicked a chunk of amber glass.

With helpless frustration, she watched him turn and really look at her car. "I hate to be the one to tell you this, princess, but your coach seems to have driven over a beer bottle."

"The fearless investigative reporter cracks another tough case."

He shook his head and turned to her. "Where's your spare?"

"I know how to change a tire, thanks."

"You wouldn't want to get grease on your pearls." He grinned, and the white flash of his teeth conjured visions of Rhett carrying Scarlett up the stairs. She shivered against a rush of lust even as she chided herself for her nonsensical romantic fantasies.

"I can manage."

"Okay. I'll just stay and watch. This should be more fun than the movie," he said, settling into a lounging pose, boots spread comfortably apart, arms crossed at the chest.

Wishing more than anything that she had her tire iron handy to brain him with, she forced a calm smile back on to her face. "I appreciate this, really I do, but I'm fine."

His gaze swept the rapidly emptying parking lot and for one crazy second she thought he worried about her safety. But that was absurd. He hoped to watch her make a fool of herself. And, darn it all, she was doing a great job.

Light from a nearby pole lamp cast his features into craggy shadows and gleamed softly on the black leather jacket. He was both menacing and reassuring, an odd combination that had her nerves snapping.

"You're not leaving, are you?"

He shook his head. "Uh-uh."

Complete exasperation flooded her body. "I don't have a spare tire."

"Darlin', the Bavarian Motor Works always include a spare." He pointed at the back of her car as if he was revealing hidden treasure. "It's in the trunk."

"No. It's on the right rear wheel." She waved the cell phone still in her hand. "I'm calling a cab."

Once more his teeth gleamed white in the night, giving him the look of a pirate with his long black hair and devil-may-care attitude. "Lock up. I'll give you a lift."

"No. Really, I..." It was pointless to keep talking when he was already striding toward his motorcycle. A couple of minutes later he was back at her side, straddling the rumbling, quivering machine.

A shiver of apprehension tickled the back of her neck at the thought of being squished against Mike's body on that thing. It was too close to her secret fantasies. And she was a firm believer that fantasies had no business morphing into reality; that was the quickest way to ruin them.

She swallowed. "Thanks anyway. I'll take a cab."

"Chicken?" he taunted.

God, yes. "No."

"Ever ridden one of these?"

She shook her head.

"Nothing to it." He winked. "It's just like falling off a bike."

She smiled weakly at the bad joke, but was certain this was a terrible idea. If she wasn't careful, she'd throw herself at him like one of his teenage groupies.

Being a sensible woman—and she was always sensible—she ought to refuse, but the dare was in his eyes, making sensible seem altogether too dull.

"All right." She forced reluctance into her tone even

as a thrill of excitement coursed through her. Would it feel as sexy as she'd imagined?

She stuffed her cell phone and car keys back into her bag and slung it around her neck.

"Come here," he said, holding up a shiny black helmet.

As he fastened the chin strap under her chin, she felt the strength in his fingers, the slight roughness of the pads of his fingertips, and shivered.

He dropped his hands as though she'd bitten him. "Get on behind me and hang on. Don't move around. Sit still and we'll do fine."

She took a breath and swung her leg over, finding footrests for her feet. She held her body stiffly back from his and, quickly realizing there was nothing else to hang on to, rested her hands as impersonally as she could on either side of his leather-jacketed waist.

He mumbled something, then the rumble beneath her increased to a roar, and they were off.

It was impossible to remain perched at the back of the slippery leather seat. As hard as she tried, she kept sliding forward until her front was plastered against his back. And the first corner had her gripping her hands all the way around his waist in a life-preserving hug.

With a shrug, she gave up the fight and slipped into the fantasy. It was a lot better to ride like this. The man in front of her was solid and warm, his muscular back much more pleasant than his mouthy front.

She could feel the shape and essence of his torso and she was frankly shocked at how strong and exciting it felt, while the machine roaring between her thighs made her feel wanton and daring.

Black hair streamed out behind him, lashing her

face and helmet, and the most vulnerable parts of her body were pressed against his, as intimate as lovers. She might as well enjoy the moment. He needn't know that desire was building in her body as the bike picked up speed.

Stars twinkled coldly in the night sky, and the sound of the rushing wind was muffled by the helmet. Traffic noise seemed far away, while she clung to her bad boy as they sped through the darkness on a long snaking road.

When at last her common sense returned, she realized the dark road they were on led, not to some erotic hideaway where Mike would carry her and make glorious, inventive love to her, but to her parents' house.

She jabbed his shoulder to get his attention. "Where are you going?" she shouted over the roar of the engine.

"Taking you home," he yelled back.

"I don't live with my parents!"

He didn't reply, and she wondered if he'd heard. But, as she was about to shout again, the roar lessened and they bumped onto the gravel shoulder.

He shot her an impatient glance over his shoulder. "And where do you live?"

She'd been so focused on the bike she hadn't thought to give him her address. And he hadn't asked, clearly assuming she still lived at home at one of the prestigious addresses that everyone in Pasqualie knew. Didn't he realize she was a grown woman?

Stowing her irritation at yet one more illustration that he didn't take her seriously, she rapidly gave him directions.

He nodded curtly, turned the bike around and once

more they sped off into the night, her fantasies trailing behind them like trodden-on, tattered ribbon.

MIKE FELT HER SOFTNESS even through his leather jacket. She clung to him as though she'd been tossed off the *Titanic* and he was the only life preserver in sight. Her breasts pressed against his back, firm but soft; her thighs wrapped his, warm and enticing. For just a second he indulged himself, imagined her in the same posture, only naked, with him facing her.

The rush of lust that slammed him damn near knocked him off the road. They rounded a corner and, as the bike tilted, she clutched him tighter, one hand settling above his heart.

With Tess wrapped around him, feeling so good he could almost believe she belonged there, he was relieved when they pulled up in front of her building. Except there was no way this dingy apartment—one of a hundred identical stucco blocks built in the seventies—was her home. What game was she playing?

"Thanks for the ride," she said, holding on to him for balance as she dismounted.

"You putting me on?" His gaze rested for a moment on her building, then shifted to her face, flushed with color from the night ride and looking a touch windblown, which only made her sexier.

"I beg your pardon?"

"*This* is where you live?"

"What's wrong with it?" Her voice lilted with curiosity.

"It's a dump."

She bristled. "It's all I can afford on my salary."

He rolled his eyes, reminding himself she was a slumming rich girl taking an adventure holiday in his world. He guessed it beat some fancy European spa, but she wasn't part of his kind of life. Never would be. "Right."

Tess yanked the helmet off her head, but he wondered why she bothered. Looked to him as if the steam coming out her ears could blow it off.

She turned to him and he expected a tongue lashing. Instead she tilted her head to one side and studied him. "Would you like to come up for coffee?"

2

Have you ever noticed the so-called "chick flicks" are about love, strong women and family? "Guy movies" are about war, bloodshed and big machines. Think about it.

MIKE'S EYES NARROWED. "You inviting me up to see your art collection?"

"No. I want to talk to you." Without giving him a chance to make any more smart remarks, or herself a chance to retract the invitation, she hauled out her keys and opened the front door of her apartment building. She wasn't certain whether he'd follow her or not as she stalked to the elevator and punched the up button then waited, wondering which tenant had had fish for dinner.

She felt him take his place at her side. They didn't speak. Not then, and not in the elevator while they watched the numbers blink until the five lit up and the scarred beige doors groaned open. She marched to Apartment 505 and fitted her key into the lock.

He followed her inside, and, as she shut the door, she wasn't at all sure she'd done a smart thing. But it was time she told him, calmly and sensibly, that she was a colleague, and a grown-up and would appreciate being treated as such.

And that's just what she was going to do, with dignity and finesse. "May I take your coat?"

"I thought you were mad at me."

So much for finesse. "I am, as a matter of fact."

"Then why are you being so polite? You want to yell? Yell. Hit me. I promise not to hit back." His eyes glinted, steely sparks in the deep blue depths that did crazy things to her pulse.

"I never yell. Your coat?"

He shrugged it off and handed it to her. The soft leather, still warm from his body, reminded her of the crazy ride, of the thrill of intimacy that still tingled in all the womanly parts of her body that had been pressed against him.

She opened the coat closet and the ill-fitting louvered door creaked, loud in the silence.

Once she'd hung the coat neatly and forced the door closed, she turned to invite him into the living room. But he was already there. Manners, she reminded herself, were not his strong suit.

She walked the few steps down the beige-carpeted hallway to the living/dining room. It wasn't much, but she'd done what she could, painting the walls a rich butter-yellow and arranging her furniture so as best to hide the stains on the wall-to-wall.

The furniture consisted of bits and pieces that she'd picked up at yard sales and flea markets and prettied up.

Mike Grundel might scoff at her car, but he'd have to admit her father's influence was nowhere to be found in her apartment. All she'd brought with her when she'd moved out on her own was her great-grandmother's bedroom suite, which had been willed to her. Maybe it was foolish pride, as her mother insisted, but Tess's independence had seemed desperately important when she set up a first home of her own.

And the truth was, she kind of liked her stuff. It was eclectic, that was for sure, and best of all she didn't worry about marring a priceless antique table with a glass of water, or staining expensive upholstery if she spilled coffee. Not that she was careless, she just felt more relaxed with furniture that wouldn't look at home in a museum.

"Coffee?" she asked brightly, fighting the urge to fidget, feeling as though her apartment had shrunk since Mike had entered it.

"Only drink it in the a.m. I'll take a beer, though, if you have it."

She shook her head slowly. "I'm all out of beer. I do have a nice Chardon— Some wine."

She couldn't decide if she disliked him more when he was scornful or when, as if now, his eyes just plain laughed at her. It felt as if she'd just failed a test. According to his rules of conduct, real reporters drank beer, she supposed.

"Wine would be great."

He was still inspecting her book collection of current paperbacks and a smattering of film star biographies when she returned with two glasses of chilled wine and, remembering how his stomach had growled earlier, a plate of cheese and crackers. He built a triple decker of cheddar and saltines and demolished it in a mouthful.

"Please, have a seat." She gestured to the old couch she'd covered with a tapestry throw. "Sorry about the mess, I wasn't expecting anyone." She swept the pile of newspapers off the coffee table and onto the floor.

Drat if his picture wasn't grinning at her from the movie section of the *Star* when she did it. And, of course, as she tried to shovel the papers out of the way, his gaze followed her movements and he caught sight of his own byline.

"So, how'd you like my *Boneblaster* review?"

"It was pretty much what I expected. As was your intelligent and sensitive commentary on *A Country Wedding.*"

He chuckled. "Bet you brought me here to steal my ideas about *You Can Keep Paris.*"

"*We'll Always Have Paris,*" she corrected automatically.

He scratched his head. "Well, I'm not saying we won't. But we should probably go there together before you start making rash pronouncements."

How did he do that? Even while he mocked her, his words carried a hint of sexual promise. An image flashed in her head of the two of them in a Paris street cafe, sipping wine. In her mind, they weren't arguing, they were holding hands, gazing at each other....

She all but slumped to the couch and sipped her very real Chardonnay, reminding herself she was in Pasqualie, not Paris. Then she sipped again, a nice big chilly gulp that shivered its way down her throat and gave her the courage to begin. "I asked you in because I want to talk to you about something."

"I wondered when we'd get to the you-being-mad-at-me part." He sat beside her, six inches closer than she would have liked, took a swig of wine and set the glass on the table. "Shoot."

But when he gazed at her, those eyes completely focused on her and with no smirk on his face or snide comment on his lips, she found it difficult to begin. For a second her breath hitched and she found herself staring at his mouth.

It was just about the sexiest mouth she'd ever seen: wide, an arrogant tilt to the corners, a bottom lip that was full and sensual. Her gaze followed a fascinating thin white scar that bisected the lower lip and traveled down to disappear into darkish stubble on his chin. She wondered what injury had left him scarred, and if she'd be able to feel it if she kissed him.

Her quick anger had passed and now she fervently wished she'd left him on the street when she'd had the chance. She didn't want to think about kissing him. She didn't want a memory of him lounging on her couch with his eyes focused on her.

"I...um, think you should take me more seriously," she said in a suddenly husky voice. *Oh, yeah. That should do it.*

"I take women like you very seriously. You're dangerous."

He was misinterpreting her, probably deliberately, but she kind of liked the part about him thinking she was dangerous. He reached out and touched her hair, sifting it through his fingers, stroking her cheek in a gesture that could be friendly or seductive. She wasn't sure how he meant the gesture, but she didn't feel friendly. She felt seduced.

She was having trouble concentrating with his face only a few inches from hers. Breathing had suddenly become an issue, and she could have sworn the pulse in his throat kicked up a notch.

Beneath heavy lids, his deep blue gaze clouded. He leaned in, so slowly she could swear he was fighting himself.

"We got off to a bad start," he said huskily, running his fingers through her hair.

"Yes. Yes, we did."

"We should start over."

"Start over?"

"Yes." His lips eased closer, hovering a mere inch from her own. She smelled the spicy, warm scent of a healthy adult predatory male. Felt his warmth and the stir of air as he moved in on her slowly.

She had plenty of time to pull away, but she didn't have the smallest desire to evade that sensual mouth. Her heart began to pound and she licked her lips in anticipation. For months this attraction had been like a quiet hum between them, never openly acknowledged, never completely ignored. Maybe it was time to see where it led. She tingled with the anticipation of his kiss.

But it didn't come.

He jerked to his feet so quickly his knee knocked the edge of the old steamer trunk she used as a coffee table, causing his wineglass to wobble.

In seconds he was leaning back against her computer desk, about as far away from her as he could get. His face was carefully expressionless, but from the way his knuckles were clamped to the desk edge, she'd guess he was deliberately holding himself in check.

"If you've got something to say, say it," he snapped, the sexy drawl gone from his tone. "I've got a review to write."

"Why don't you like me?" Argh. She could have bitten off her tongue the minute she spoke. He'd rattled her so she couldn't think straight. Her voice sounded both wistful and peevish—about as mature as a bullied six-year-old.

Whatever he'd been expecting, it wasn't that. He rubbed a hand across his face, grimacing. "Who says I don't like you?"

Her mouth would have dropped open had she not taken deportment lessons at private school. "You were just about to kiss me, then you leaped to the other side of the room."

A huffy sigh escaped his lips. "Do you know how many media jobs come open in this part of the country?"

Her brow creased. What did that have to do with anything? "Not many."

"You're damn right. Not many. And yet you, with no experience, nothing to recommend you but your father's influence and money, scoop one of the plums when there are seasoned reporters out there working as car salesmen and construction workers to support their families."

"I graduated top of my journalism class. I—"

"Journalism class." He made it sound like something you'd step around in the street. "You don't learn about news sitting in a classroom. You put your nose to the ground and start sniffing. You wouldn't recognize news if it bit you in the ass."

Indignation, swift and fierce, consumed her. "I can't help it that my father's rich. But this is *my career* and I will not be patronized by a slob who thinks *Boneblaster III* is great art."

She wanted to tell him about her other job offers, but that would involve explaining why she'd returned to her hometown, and she wasn't sure she *could* explain it.

It was as though she needed to prove to everyone—
mostly herself—that she could become a top reporter
on her own. It wouldn't have meant as much in another city. For some reason, she had to prove herself
here in Pasqualie.

If she could convince the arrogant but talented Mike
Grundel that she was a real journalist then maybe
she'd finally taste success.

"This is discrimination, you know," she said to him.
"You made up your mind without giving me a
chance. And—" she narrowed her eyes, going for the
jugular "—if you're such a great newshound, what are
you doing on the entertainment page?"

He flushed darkly. "That's different. I had a source
choke on me."

"I can imagine how that feels. And I want you to
know I understand how circumstances could put you
in that position and that I don't hold it against you in
the least." *Was she good or what?* "I have an open
mind."

After a short struggle with himself, he grinned. "I
give you this round. But I'm telling you, you're in a
tough business. You can't take the heat, get out of the
newsroom."

Ooh. She was going to get a story so hot it would
burn his feet as he raced to catch up. She set her wineglass down with a snap. He was always challenging
her, one way or another. This time she decided to pick
up the gauntlet and slap his face with it. "I will make
you a bet."

"A bet?" He straightened and leaned forward, his
mouth quirking.

"Yes. I bet you that I will have a front page story
printed before you will."

His eyes sparkled with challenge. "I play to win, princess."

"Then you'll have no objection to taking my bet. Hard news story only, on the front page. Whoever gets it first, wins."

"What are the stakes?"

"I..." She hadn't thought of that. She was impressed enough that she'd come up with the idea in the biggest display of bravado in her life. "I don't know."

A sly grin lit his face. "Tell you what. Whoever wins cooks the other one dinner."

"Whoever *wins* cooks? That doesn't seem fair."

"The loser has to eat it."

She wrinkled her brow, getting a bad feeling about this. "And what does the loser have to eat?"

"Crow."

She might have known he'd pick something gross and juvenile. "Crow."

"That's the bet, babe. Take it or leave it." He was heading for the door as he said it, as though he really didn't care.

"Oh, I'll take it." She rose and followed him, to find him already shrugging into his coat. "I'm not afraid of you."

He put his hand on the doorknob then suddenly turned. "Maybe you should be," he said, and pulled her into his arms.

Surprise and a tiny spurt of panic shot through her as his mouth took hers. It felt as though he folded her into the kiss. Bending her here, arching her there, as he fit their bodies together. His lips covered hers with passion, firmness and a hint of frustration.

As the panic and surprise ebbed, desire took their place. She felt the quick splurge of pleasure at being in the arms of a man who knew exactly what he wanted. And exactly what she needed.

The quiet hum built to a roar as blood pounded in her ears, echoing the rhythm of her heart. With a moan, she gave in to it, in to him, welcoming the onslaught of emotions as his tongue plunged inside her mouth with more demand than finesse.

She'd been kissed with finesse plenty of times, but never with such raw, unabashed wanting, and she found herself responding ravenously. Her hands clutched his shoulders, then, unable to resist the temptation, dove into his hair, pulling him closer against her.

She met him need for need, tangled in the warmth and strength of him, wanting more, pressing closer. He felt so good, so hard and male, even though she was dimly aware that this was a very bad idea.

He must have concluded the same thing, for he eased her out of the kiss with a lot more finesse than he'd plunged into it, softening and toying, giving her a moment to tamp down the lust that spiked through her. It wasn't easy to back away when she felt as though something cataclysmic had just occurred.

When at last he pulled away, she stared at him with blank shock, his own surprise mirrored back at her.

"Oh, my," she said, raising a hand to her heart. "This could complicate things."

He opened the door and stepped out into the hall. "Count on it."

3

What is it with the French and sex? They spend so much time talking about it...

MIKE'S FINGERS PAUSED over the keys. Thinking about sex had the image of Tess popping into his head. He'd almost tugged the kite all the way in last night. It had been one of the toughest things he'd ever done to walk away from her. She'd been hot, and sweet, and willing, making him want her with a fierceness that stunned him. No woman had affected him that way in a long while. Maybe ever.

He cursed under his breath.

There were stars in her eyes. He knew the type. She equated sex with love, love with marriage, and marriage with his-and-her golf carts at the club.

He shuddered at the thought. Tess Elliot was most definitely not his type. If Pasqualie had royalty, she was it. A distant and cool Ice Princess, as beautiful as she was unattainable.

Thanks but no thanks. He liked his sex hot, sweaty, with no hard feelings when he was on his way. Not a commitment in sight.

She was something, though, and damn if she wasn't tougher than he'd figured. A little friendly rivalry over a news story should put one more sorely needed barrier between them. One more reason for him not to jump her most delectable aristocratic bones. She'd thrown out quite a challenge, and he was looking forward to cooking up that crow and making her eat it.

A silent chuckle shook him. He was an excellent cook, a fact not many people knew. It had started when he was a kid fending for himself when the old man was on a bender. His mom was long gone by then. Mike sometimes wondered if she was a good cook and he'd inherited the gene from her. Hard to tell since she'd left before he had started school. Whatever the reason, he'd taken to the kitchen and figured his battered copy of *Joy of Cooking* had scored him a lot more action than his much less battered copy of *Joy of Sex*.

He'd cook up a nice quail or a Cornish game hen, sauced and stuffed to perfection. And he'd make Tess clean her plate. Watching her choke down the "crow" would add a bonus to getting his real job back.

He shouldn't have taken Tess's bet; he was an experienced journalist with a few years under his belt and a keen nose for scandal. She was a society princess who'd spent her life pampered and sheltered from all the good stuff that made front-page headlines. If she hadn't got under his skin with her comment about his demotion, he wouldn't have accepted her challenge.

Oh, hell. Who was he kidding? Of course he would have. Saving spoiled little rich girls from their own foolishness wasn't his job.

He stood. Getting his job back was his job—and maybe the princess's little bet was just the poke he needed to make it happen.

Leaving his review half completed, he strode to the managing editor's office and barged in. "Mel, you've got to give me a break from these movie reviews, I can't stand it anymore."

Mel glanced up from her computer and ran her fingers through brutally short white-blond hair, causing further disarray. "Just the man I want to see."

His heart leaped. *Yes*, she was putting him back on news.

"Take a look at these." She riffled through the piles of paper on her desk until she found what she was looking for. "The results of our latest reader survey. Check out page six."

Mike took the paper-clipped bundle and flipped. Readers randomly surveyed were asked, "Do you read Mike Grundel's movie reviews?" and "Do you agree with him?"

He shrugged. "So what? Half the people like what I write and half the people hate it."

"Come on, Mikey, look again." Mel's frequent cigarette breaks had worn off most of her lipstick, leaving a red pencil line around her thin lips. Those lips were smiling—always a bad sign.

"For what?"

"Look at the readership figures. Ninety-eight percent of those surveyed said they 'always' or 'often' read your movie column. And check out the reader responses. Who likes you?"

Mike glanced through the material again and made the obvious connection. "Men like my stuff, women don't."

"Women don't just dislike your stuff, hon. They hate it." Her scratchy two-pack-a-day voice resonated with glee.

He tossed the papers back onto her desk. "You can't

please everybody. Assign the reviews to another reporter. I'll go back to news."

"You're still missing the point. Women read your reviews every week to remind themselves that men are pigs. Men read the same reviews and start beating their chests. You probably cause as many arguments in Pasqualie households as sex and money. That, my boy, is controversy. And that sells papers."

"Look, Mel. I know I blew it on the Ty Cadman story. I thought my source would come forward when I needed him."

Her lips tightened and the smile went south. "And I thought you had other sources. You made us all look like idiots." She ground her teeth audibly. "I hate printing apologies."

"But that bribery story was true."

"There was no story without other sources to back it up and you know that."

"Okay, so I put my tail between my legs and did movie reviews like a good boy—"

"And they saved your butt. Today, in the management meeting, was the first time Joel didn't ask why I haven't fired you yet."

If the publisher wanted him fired, he'd been in deeper water than he thought. He owed Mel, but he was still the best reporter she had, and he was wasted on the stupid movie beat. "I've paid my dues. Come on. I've got to have a break."

She turned back to the computer.

"Don't make me beg."

Her fingers started flying over the keys.

"Okay, okay. I'm begging you here, Mel."

She turned back to him. "Well, now we know everybody reads your reviews I'm putty in your hands."

She dug through the pile again and handed him more paper. "Here."

He stared down at the letter and attached tickets, horror buckling his stomach. He glanced up at Mel to see if she was joking, but there was no grin on her face. "Opera tickets?"

"That's right. You'll be taking in the opening night of *La Traviata* at the new opera house."

His tie felt too tight. And he wasn't wearing a tie. "But that's Cadman's place."

"Right again. Built by upstanding citizen Ty Cadman for the people of Pasqualie. There's a story for you, Tiger. Go get it."

"But we don't do stories like this," he argued feebly.

Her voice was granite-hard. "We do when we're kissing up."

Mike left Mel's office before he did something stupid, such as quit his job. He wasn't a quitter, never had been. And besides, he had a score to settle with Mr. Tyrone Cadman. Maybe he'd been too quick to go to press, but the story was true, he knew it in his bones.

Mike wasn't leaving Pasqualie, or the *Star*, until he had the story. Airtight, watertight, sue-proof. Then, once he had his reputation back, he'd be out of this backwater faster than you could say "civic corruption."

But first he had to get Cadman.

THE CAVERNOUS marble foyer buzzed with talk and restrained laughter. Champagne glasses clinked among small, elegantly dressed groups. Tess shivered, feeling her shoulders begin to goose bump in the strapless evening gown.

Harrison Peabody placed a tuxedo-clad arm around

her shoulders and squeezed. "Would you like me to get your wrap?"

"No, thanks." But his hand was gone and Harrison was already on his way to fetch it. Harrison was one of her oldest friends, but the man made a doormat look as if it had backbone.

While Harrison was gone, Tess listened to the string quartet, savored the opening-night excitement and the see-and-be-seen comings and goings of the well-dressed crème de la crème of Pasqualie society.

Her parents were across the foyer, both looking elegant and successful, in a group that included Harrison Peabody's parents. She caught her mother's eye and they exchanged a wave. Tess was conscious of conflicting feelings. She loved her parents and admired them, but didn't want to think she was looking across the foyer at her future.

A waiter offered her a tray and she took a flute of champagne with a sigh. Maybe she shouldn't have come back to Pasqualie.

Feeling herself under scrutiny, Tess turned and her breath seemed to catch in her throat.

Mike Grundel in a tuxedo?

She gave a discreet tug to the underwire bra responsible for her cleavage; maybe it was too tight. She had to be hallucinating.

As she watched, Mike ran a finger under his black bow tie as though he was also having trouble breathing. Their gazes remained locked and she wondered if, after the steamy kiss they'd shared the other night, she'd started making him appear, rather like a particularly sexy genie, whenever she needed to remind herself that she was young, with her own life to lead. If he presented her with three wishes, she wondered where she'd begin.

Then he sauntered toward her and she noticed the black motorcycle helmet swinging from his hand, assuring her that he was flesh and blood and no hallucination. Beneath the formal elegance of the tuxedo the cocky Mike showed through. He hadn't tied his hair back, but left it to swing, black and slightly curly at the ends, against the satin lapels. A diamond stud glittered in his ear to suit the formality of the evening. In spite of herself, Tess found a smile tugging at her lips.

Those blue, blue eyes of his were traveling from her satin pumps, up her legs, over the silk sheath dress. They hovered briefly at her underwired cleavage before making their way to her face. Their kiss had changed things, she thought, noting the frankly carnal expression in his eyes. That unspoken sexual attraction was out in the open now. She wondered what they'd do about it.

"Wow," he said. "You look fantastic."

If he started being nice to her, this man could be dangerous. "Thanks. You clean up pretty well yourself." With his panther-like grace and dark good looks, he was both exotic and exciting. He had the blue eyes, glossy black hair and a certain tousled poetic look of the Irish, but the lean cheeks and tawny skin of a Spanish pirate. The combination was mouthwatering and just a little scary.

"So, you're covering the opening, too," he said. "Maybe you can help me out with my French."

"*La Traviata* is in Italian." She said it automatically, before she noted the disturbing twinkle in Mike's eye. She was beginning to wonder if he was quite as primitive as he made out. "But I'm not covering the opera, we've already done our story. I'm here socially."

He rolled his gaze to the lofty domed ceiling. "You're one of the benefactors?"

"My, um, friend is."

At that moment her friend reappeared across the foyer, holding the silk shawl that matched her dress. And with him was Ty Cadman. Like everybody else in town, Tess knew Mike had tried to bring Cadman down and failed. His allegations of an unfair bidding process and secret payoffs in the construction of this very building had been fascinating reading.

Even more interesting was the apology the *Star* was forced to print after the one quoted source, a disgruntled competitor, claimed he was misquoted. According to her father, only that retraction and Mike's demotion had saved the *Star* from a libel case.

But Tess had known Mr. Cadman most of her life, and she didn't think it was civic-mindedness or a generous spirit that had caused him to let the newspaper off so lightly.

She wondered why he hadn't sued the paper. Was he, perhaps, more unwilling to go to court and let all the facts emerge than he had let on?

He'd tried first to have Mike fired, but the *Star* had, in its way, stood by their top news reporter, demoting him instead. Mr. Cadman had had to content himself with knowing he'd humiliated the man who'd set out to humiliate him.

The reporter in question stiffened as he, too, noted who was coming toward them. All the humor drained out of his eyes.

Tess's stomach tightened. If she'd been him, she would have slunk away to avoid a confrontation;

Mike, of course, lived for confrontation. He moved a step closer to her, whether to annoy Mr. Cadman or in an unconscious protective gesture, she had no idea.

His nearness certainly had an effect on her. He was so near she could feel the heat coming off his body, smell the dry-cleaning solvent on his rented tux, count each line of disdain that carved itself onto his face.

Harrison and Mr. Cadman chatted easily as they approached. When the latter spotted Mike, she saw him pause and an ugly look flashed across his narrow face.

An uncomfortable pause fell over the group. Harrison Peabody took refuge in Tess's silk shawl, fussing it around her shoulders.

Ty Cadman paused a stride away from Mike. Animosity crackled like dry lightning. She was certain she felt her blood pressure rising. She probably could have eased over the difficult moment but she chose, instead, to watch the confrontation.

"Seen any good movies lately?" Mr. Cadman sneered.

"I heard Saul Feldman got a plum job in your Seattle office," Mike countered. Saul Feldman was the source who'd changed his story. If Mike had kept tabs on his source, he must still be digging. Still hoping to bring Cadman down.

Cadman glanced up from under perfect silver eyebrows. "Don't believe every rumor you hear. It could get you in trouble." Then he turned and gave Tess an avuncular smile. She blinked at the blinding brightness of his smile. He'd had his teeth bleached. Straightened, too, she was certain. He turned his back on Mike as though the reporter didn't exist. "You're looking lovely tonight, Tess. You're turning into a beauty like your mother."

"Thank you, Mr. Cadman. The opera house is lovely. I understand the marble was brought in specially from Italy." She was gushing. She ought to throw in a few snarly journalistic jabs of her own. But somehow it was tough to snarl at a man who'd known her since she wore diapers. Besides, there was enough non-verbal snarling going on between Mike and Mr. Cadman, and it put her nerves on edge.

"Yes. It's Carerra marble. I like the best. Well, enjoy the performance." He glanced once more at Mike. "Don't hesitate to call my office if you need to check any facts." And with that Parthian shot, he strode off to chat with the next group.

She introduced the two men still with her. They shook hands and the suppressed amusement in Mike's eyes told her he thought her pale-skinned, pale-eyed escort was perfect for her.

She wanted to scream, "It's not a date!"

"It sure is a beautiful building," Harrison said with hearty joviality, almost wiping his brow in relief that the unpleasant confrontation was over.

She helped Harrison out by rolling the ball back. "Yes, isn't it? The arches and pillars give a very neo-classic look."

Harrison took a nervous sip of champagne before coming up with another conversational gem. "I wonder if he'll use the same construction team for his wilderness retreat."

"Wilderness retreat?" she murmured politely. She had no idea what Harrison was talking about. Ty Cadman was the most urban person she knew. He loved people, parties, nightlife, dining, theater. He certainly didn't strike her as the wilderness type.

"He's bought land on Pasqualie River. Lots of it. He's a nut for privacy."

Pasqualie River? Tess had hiked the area; it was a haven for outdoor types, bird and wildlife watchers, and guys who liked to wade up to their thighs in the river to go fly-fishing. It was also thick with mosquitoes in summer, wet and boggy in winter. Why would a man who hated the outdoors buy a wilderness retreat?

Tess could feel a tingling sensation at the end of her nose; it always happened when she was onto a story. Maybe she didn't have a lot of hard news experience, but she'd earned her spot at the top of her journalism class by following her instincts.

She opened her lips to question Harrison further, then shut them tight. She shot a glance under her lashes at Mike, but he was staring thoughtfully over to the other side of the marble foyer where Mr. Cadman was now chatting with her parents and Harrison's. Presumably Mike hadn't heard Harrison, or didn't know Mr. Cadman well enough to think such behavior odd.

An idea, startling in its brilliance, occurred to her. What if she could scoop super-reporter Mike Grundel on his own story? Perhaps this proposed wilderness retreat was worth investigating. If Mr. Cadman was a crook, whether he'd seen her in diapers or not, she'd have no hesitation in uncovering the truth.

Gleeful butterflies were line-dancing in her chest.

While she was wondering what kind of vegetables one served with crow, she heard her name called. She came back to earth to find one of the most beautiful women on earth, and her best friend, Caroline Kushner, and her husband, Jonathon, the publisher of the *Standard*, approaching.

Caro, a retired supermodel, hugged Tess warmly even though they'd seen each other only the day before when Caro was in working on a fashion story for the paper.

Tess pulled out of Caro's expensively scented embrace to find Jon and Mike lobbing insults at each other in one of those male bonding rituals she never grasped.

Only Harrison Peabody seemed not to know anyone, so she introduced him to the group.

It had felt strange at first when she went to work for the *Standard*, knowing the publisher was married to her best friend. But Tess had relaxed when she learned Jon stayed out of the editorial department's way and never interfered with personnel issues. He was a brilliant administrator and savvy marketer who'd managed to make an already-successful paper thrive. He owned a couple of cable and radio stations, as well, but his heart was obviously in the *Standard*. What heart he could spare from Caro.

Tess wasn't jealous of her friend's stunning looks, or her professional success. But when Jonathon gazed at his wife, Tess experienced a sharp twinge of envy. She wondered what it would be like to have a man look at her that way, and very much hoped she'd find out. Caro had retired from professional modeling and now spent her time writing for the *Standard*'s fashion section, which she did as a favor to Jon, and lending her name and considerable energy to charity projects, which she did for love.

"How's the fund-raising going for the children's after-school art program?" Tess asked.

"Great. Thanks for writing the media release."

Since Jon and Mike were currently deeply into sports talk, and Harrison was struggling to keep up, Tess said in a low voice, "Are Jon and Mike friends?"

Caro laughed. "It surprised me, too. They're best friends."

"But, how did..." Tess didn't know how to phrase the question.

"How did a kid born with a silver spoon and a kid who's dad was an unemployed drunk end up friends? Sports. Baseball. They both made the city team. The way Jon tells it, they went head to head right away, bloodied noses, and ended up friends."

"And to think we bonded with no bruises or bleeding. Amazing."

At the signal indicating the performance was about to start, the group broke up and went to their respective seats. From her position in one of the private boxes, Tess had a great view of Mike, head back against the seat, his eyes closed.

He could be in rapt contemplation of the music, but she had a feeling he'd fallen asleep.

She'd learned a couple of things tonight that had the muscles in her stomach clenching with excitement. One was that Mr. Cadman was up to something—what it was she didn't know, but she was determined to find out.

The other was that Mike Grundel looked fantastic in a tux.

She'd have to tell him to wear it when she cooked him dinner.

4

Once in a while a movie comes along that revisits the golden age of witty repartee, when women were glamorous and men actually noticed....

TESS SIGHED, and her mind wandered from her movie review. She'd been glamorous at the opera house opening, and Mike Grundel had definitely noticed. Of course, his witty repartee was more like a bloodbath with broadswords, but still, he intrigued her with all his contradictions.

Perhaps if he hadn't kissed her the other night she could get him out of her mind. But that was impossible. That kiss had changed things, and she didn't know what she wanted to do about it. Nothing for now. She had a career to get off the ground, and no sexy bad boy was going to stop her.

She hoped.

Mmm. His kisses were a bit like his movie reviews, outrageous and yet compelling. She got shivery just thinking about how his glances had scorched her at the opera opening, and how the civilized veneer of a tux only emphasized the uncivilized male animal beneath. It made her blood sizzle wondering how all that elemental energy would feel if completely unleashed on her. Still, she needed to win the bet and to establish her career more than she needed a complicated affair with a competitor.

First she'd feed Mike Grundel crow, then she'd think about seducing him. She chuckled. In the meantime there was the small matter of scooping him at his own story.

She thought about Harrison's comment as she approached city hall shortly after it opened Monday morning. On the way home from the opera house she'd grilled Harrison, but he'd only overheard somebody talking about Ty Cadman's wilderness retreat on Pasqualie River. He couldn't remember who'd said it or where he found out about it. As a source, Harrison was just this side of pathetic. He wasn't great at paying attention, but he didn't usually get things wrong, either, and she decided his hazy information was worth following up.

She wondered what, if anything, a supposed wilderness retreat had to do with bribery on a civic building project. She'd lain awake last night trying to find some connection, but she'd come up blank. According to Mike's discredited story, Cadman had obtained an advance peek at the rival bids to construct the opera center. It had then been a simple matter for him to come in as the low bidder. The mayor's name was never mentioned in the *Star* article, but everyone in town knew he and Mr. Cadman had been friends for years. Tess's father couldn't stand the mayor, and only tolerated Cadman, and her father was a pretty smart man.

Light fog caressed her cheeks with cool, dewy fingers as she reached the door of the squat public building. If she could verify that Cadman had purchased land by the river she'd have the most important fact to back up Harrison's story. If not, then maybe her tingling nose merely indicated she was coming down with a cold.

The roar of a motorcycle engine shattered the foggy silence, and she paused to watch a misty black form speed out of the adjacent alley.

The rider glanced to the left before making a right turn and she glimpsed his face. It was Mike.

Her heart jerked crazily.

She stood there, wondering what she'd do if he saw her and offered her a ride. Knowing she'd love to ride off into the mist and let him take her...

But he didn't even see her. As he disappeared into the fog, and her heart rate returned to normal, she wondered what he was doing in the neighborhood.

She was still wondering as she made her way to the property registry desk and approached a clerk standing at the counter.

"Help you?" the woman asked in a bored voice.

"Yes. I'm interested in property on Pasqualie River."

"Did they discover gold there?" The woman stared at her, no longer sounding the least bit bored. "You're the second person who's asked me about Pasqualie River this morning."

"Really?" she said through gritted teeth. So Mike *had* picked up on Harrison's remark the other night. Double damn. "May I see the property records?"

"Second floor."

"Thanks." Tess ran up the single flight of stairs and entered glass doors with Land Use/Planning stenciled on them in black lettering. A large survey map of the area hung on a wall, the incorporated area of Pasqualie in pink. She started with the map, using her finger to trace the river, her memory conjuring the properties she traced. There was the city's waterfront park, with its riverfront boardwalk, picnic grounds, a play area for the kids. A little farther out, farmland, lush and green in the summer with livestock grazing contentedly beside the river, then the area she'd always thought of as wilderness, though it, too, was parceled and owned.

She marked down the tax parcel numbers of all the properties adjacent to the river then, with the help of a clerk, found herself with a box of microfiche and a reader. As she juggled from screen to screen, squinting to read the ownership information for each parcel of land, she cursed the municipal officials that Pasqualie didn't get with the new millennium and put all this stuff on computer.

She scribbled herself a simple map and wrote in the registered property owners. The largest block of property out in the wilderness area was owned by a numbered company. Cadman's? But many smaller properties adjacent to it had recently changed hands. And the new information was on computer. Mr. Cadman didn't show up as a new owner, but Harrison's mother, Margaret Peabody, did. A few of the other names of new owners were familiar as well—three had been at the opera opening. Now that was interesting.

Deep in thought, she drove to the *Standard* building. Once at her desk, she pored over her list more carefully.

By far the largest property owner, apart from the numbered company, was an organization called Bald is Beautiful. Their land bordered that owned by the numbered company.

Was this Cadman's land? Was the name a private joke? But he had a thick head of hair that was always meticulously groomed—she couldn't imagine a man with his ego making that sort of joke on a property document.

Deep in thought, she drove to the *Standard* building. Once at her desk, she pored over her list more carefully.

Around her she heard the low sigh of running computers, the jangling of phones, and the back-and-forth kibitzing of reporters between stories or waiting for calls.

"What's another word for 'bereaved'?" sighed Anton from the obit side of the desk.

"Grieving?"

"I used that in the last paragraph."

"Sorrowful?"

"Thanks," he said, sounding sorrowful himself.

"Bald is Beautiful, what are you?" she wondered out loud.

"An engo. Out at the uni," Steve Ackerman replied.

"A university environmental group?" She stared at Steve. He was a solid ten on the hunk-o-meter, but he had a reputation of scoring a lot lower in the brains department. Of course, he'd chosen to move to sports from hard news, which pretty much confirmed the rumor in her mind.

Steve paused at her desk and took off his glasses to polish them on his polo shirt. "Their mission is to protect bald eagle habitats."

"Are you sure?"

He grinned. "I dated a B.I.B. member for a while. She used to drag me out in the woods with binoculars. I'm sure."

"Thanks, Steve. Ah, this girlfriend, could you get me in touch with her?"

He pushed his glasses back on his nose. "Sorry. I never go back. Can't even remember her last name."

Were all men in the newspaper business like Mike? "Do you remember her first name?"

"Sure. It was Lenore...Lorraine...Laine...?" He shrugged as if it didn't matter all that much. "Something with an *L*."

"Like Loser," she muttered under her breath as Steve continued on his way.

She had no idea what this latest piece of intelligence meant or, coming from Steve, if it would turn out to be correct. Still, it was the only lead she had, and he'd mentioned that the group operated out of the university. Even if the L-woman wasn't around, perhaps someone on campus would know about the organization. She jumped up and grabbed her bag, telling Anton, "If anyone asks, I'm taking an early lunch."

Bypassing the elevator she took the stairs at a trot.

This whole thing didn't make any sense. Ty Cadman wouldn't get involved in anything so earthy as wildlife conservation, and yet Harrison Peabody claimed he owned land near the river. Harrison's mother certainly had land there. Tess rubbed the end of her nose. Should she start with the Peabodys or the university?

Once in her car, she hesitated then headed toward Pasqualie University.

An hour later she knew more about bald eagles than she ever wanted to know and was twenty-five bucks poorer, having done her bit to save the big birds' diminishing habitat.

Fortunately, B.I.B. had an office in the basement of

the student union building and she'd been able to talk to the student manning the desk.

"They breed near rivers, and development is destroying their breeding grounds," the long-haired ascetic named Jeremy Dennis told her. "That area of Pasqualie River is a spawning ground for salmon and is surrounded by western red cedar, alders and mature cottonwood. Eagles love to perch in cottonwood in winter and they love pigging out on salmon at spawning time."

"Oh, my. That must be something to see."

He nodded. "Originally, Bald is Beautiful was set up to support the work of Eugene Butterworth."

"The painter?" Her eyes widened in surprise. "That's right, he lived around here." And his art had become very collectible. Her father had a Butterworth hanging in his office—a doe and fawn drinking from a stream. She'd always loved that picture.

"He was a naturalist as well as a painter and wanted to preserve wildlife habitat. A professor here at the university started Bald is Beautiful while Butterworth was still alive. When he died, he left his paintings and papers to B.I.B. Now, we also operate a land trust. We raise money to buy up land along the Pasqualie." He flipped a straggly brown braid over his shoulder. "Sometimes we luck out and the owners donate the land."

Her nose felt as if it was smoking. If she could prove Ty Cadman was behind the numbered company that owned the chunk of land on the river, she had a really juicy developer versus the environment story on her hands. And if the legendary Eugene Butterworth was part of it, this could have national significance.

Trying to keep the excitement out of her voice, she

said, "I notice your land borders a riverfront section owned by a numbered company. Do you know anything about that?"

Jeremy shifted in his seat, and offered her an apologetic, toothy grin. "Yeah, but I'm not allowed to tell. Sorry. I know you're a member and everything now, but you're also the press. You know."

"Sure." She smiled at him while her back molars ground together. "I understand. I'd love to do a feature article on the group sometime. Maybe we can raise awareness of the issues, get people behind the project."

"Oh, yeah. That'd be great."

"Is there anything you can tell me about that land?"

He fidgeted with his pen. "It's okay. That land. The owners are on our side."

She almost fell out of her chair. Could wildlife habitat preservation and Cadman possibly go together? It was worth investigating.

"Do you know Ty Cadman?"

Jeremy gazed at her with a puzzled frown. "I read about him in the papers sometimes. Sure."

"I was just wondering if he was a B.I.B. benefactor?"

Jeremy's protuberant blue gaze fixed on her face as though she was a few carob chips short of a full granola bar. "The developer? You think he'd support habitat conservation?"

"I know he's a big philanthropist." She shrugged. "If he's not already contributing, I could talk to him."

"Well, I guess we take anybody's money. I'll check the membership list." He pulled a dog-eared sheaf of papers out of a desk drawer. "Computers are down," he explained to Tess as he flipped through the document, while she scanned names from upside down.

"No." Jeremy shook his head. "There's no Cadman here." He dug out a pen. "Might as well add your name while I have this in front of me."

While he flipped from C to E on the list, she kept scanning names. Lots were handwritten, which made them tough to decipher. "Have the computers been down a long time?"

"One computer. Almost a week, I guess."

She felt her brows pull together at the number of penned-and penciled-in names. "Did you get that many new members in a week?"

He flipped through the list. "Our secretary is a volunteer and only comes in when she gets time between classes. She was probably a week behind already. But, yeah. We've had a lot of new members in the last month."

"Did you do some kind of membership drive?"

"No." He shrugged. "These things come and go."

She almost asked if the Peabodys were among the new members, but she didn't want to push her luck. Besides, she was planning to visit with Margaret Peabody later; she'd ask her.

After thanking Jeremy for his time and promising to do a feature to help raise awareness of the organization she'd now joined, she left, excitement churning in her belly and her mind full of questions.

She glanced at her watch on her way back to her car and decided she had time to drop in on Mrs. Peabody if she skipped lunch entirely.

When she looked up again, a very familiar figure was stalking down the sidewalk toward her, his black hair loose and sexy the way she liked it. His jeans sat low on his hips, boots clacking with purpose on the pavement. Her stomach plummeted faster than an eagle going after prey. Once could have been coincidence. Twice? Uh-uh. Damn, damn, damn. They *were* after the same story.

Mike Grundel caught sight of her and halted with a jerk, blue eyes narrowing on her face.

"Registering for your freshman year?" she asked sweetly, trying to ignore the hammering of her heart at the sight of all that rugged maleness. A breeze tossed strands of glossy hair against the open collar of his denim shirt.

"Trolling for chicks. You?"

She gestured to the massive stone library across University Boulevard. "Catching up on some light reading."

His gaze softened, seemed to linger on her lips. If he really had come to troll for chicks, he was going about it the right way.

She smiled at him, trying to ignore the little sizzle he'd ignited in her belly. She had a mission and she couldn't forget that. "And I might enroll in a cooking course. For exotic fowl."

Those dangerously sexy eyes began to twinkle with reluctant amusement. He must realize, as she had, that they were following up the same lead. "The bald eagle is an endangered species."

"As you're about to discover, it's been upgraded to threatened. Besides, I was thinking of cooking something common enough to appeal to you. Something black that goes caw."

"You've got plenty of nerve, I'll give you that." He lifted his hand to her face and tucked a windblown lock of hair behind her ear, sending tingles shivering down her spine. "But this is *my* story."

She tried to ignore the fluttering of her nerve endings as his fingers skimmed the top of her ear and seemed to pause at the pulse point just behind the lobe. Her voice emerged as breathless as the breeze. "And what story is that?"

Looking as baffled as she was beginning to feel, he muttered, "Damned if I know," and headed through the door.

It was almost midnight when Tess's intercom buzzed. She rubbed her eyes, blurry from staring at a computer screen while her random notes stared back at her. She'd searched the Internet and found loads of information on bald eagles, noted the B.I.B. site could use some updating, and discovered nothing that helped with her current story. At least nothing that linked Cadman to any of it.

No one had been home at the Peabodys' so that was another lead that had stalled.

Her buzzer sounded again and she rose. Probably a wrong number, she thought as she answered.

"Tess, it's me. Mike."

"Mike Grundel?" It wasn't as if she was up to her armpits in guys called Mike, but she couldn't imagine why her archrival was calling on her at midnight. Unless...

"Yeah. Can I come up?"

She glanced down at herself, decent enough in sweats, but hardly in the mood for sexy-as-sin gentleman callers. "Why?"

"I have a proposition."

She chuckled, even as a rush of heat swept over her. "At least you're honest."

"Not that kind." His voice crackled over the intercom. "I can't tell you from here. Come on, let me up."

It was a really bad idea. He was sexier than Clark Gable, sneakier than a calorie and about as resistible as Swiss chocolate.

She pushed the button to let him in.

5

Saw a flick last night where a dude in a monkey suit asked a woman if she liked her wine as dry as her conversation. Get real. What happened to, "Hey, babe. Let's do the nasty."

TOO IMPATIENT TO WAIT for the creaky old elevator, Mike bounded up the stairs and banged on Tess's door, out of breath and stewing.

"Let's make a deal," he said the moment she opened the door.

"And good evening to you, too."

How any woman managed to look cool and sophisticated in a pair of gray sweatpants and a University of Western Washington hoodie was beyond him, but Tess did. Nothing could disguise the air of culture, expensive education and moneyed background. In this dump of an apartment she looked like a fancy porcelain doll in a dime store.

She also looked tired and frustrated, which he could totally relate to, and so kissable he stuck his hands in his jeans' pockets and stomped past her out of harm's way.

She sent him one of her superior smirks. "Please, come right in."

"Cut the finishing school crap. You want to do a deal or don't you?"

The door shut with a snap. She gestured to her couch and turned on another lamp, as if maybe she didn't want to be alone with him in the dark. Smart lady. "What kind of deal?"

He ignored the couch, too wired to sit. Instead he paced her small living room. He had a really bad feeling in his gut that he was losing perspective. That this was one of his worst ideas ever. And there were quite a few to choose from—kissing Tess the other night being the chart-topper.

He watched from under his brows as she headed for her kitchenette, distracted by the sway of her hips in the softly clinging sweats.

Once again, as he had too often this week, he recalled the way she'd felt on his bike with her arms and legs wrapped around him and her chest jammed against his back. Good didn't even begin to describe it. She'd felt more than good, almost as though she belonged there. And that didn't come close to the way she'd felt in his arms, which had his early warning system on full alert. He shook his head as though he could shake his stupidity right out his ears, so riled he could barely think straight.

He heard the sucking pull of a fridge door opening, a metallic clink and then she reappeared with two bottles of beer. She held them at chest height and after thinking about how good that beer would taste, he noticed the perky sway of her breasts under the cotton—he was certain there was nothing between the sweatshirt and her naked flesh.

The bottle was slick with condensation when he took it with a brief word of thanks. He drank deeply, giving himself an internal cold shower as he swallowed.

"You said something about a deal?" she prompted, perching on the chair at her desk. A small desk light was switched on, illuminating an open notebook. The computer was humming, but the screen was turned off.

"Working on a movie review?" he asked.

Her eyes flickered. "Not exactly."

He tapped the bottle against his teeth. The hell with it. Stupidity hadn't killed him yet. "Did you get in to see the Peabodys?"

She sent him a long, cool Grace Kelly look. "What kind of deal are we talking about?" Her voice was just as cool.

Frustration made him blurt, "The Peabodys wouldn't talk to me."

"They don't know what they're missing. All that charm and wit."

"Yeah. I used so much charm, Peabody called Mel, my managing editor."

She bit her plump lower lip and a crease appeared between her brows. Even she could figure out that complaints about him from Ty Cadman's dear friends wouldn't help his career. "Do you want me to talk to them?"

He was momentarily diverted. "Would you?"

She shrugged. "Yes." Humor lit deep in her eyes like a candle in a winter window. "I can't win the bet if you get fired."

"Then you might want to speak to Mel. She tore so many strips off me...I felt like that peeling mummy in the horror flick last week."

She laughed, showing glossy pearl-white teeth and just a hint of pink tongue.

He shuddered. He'd taken knockouts in the ring

that weren't as brutal as Mel's verbal lashing. "If I so much as *read* the news section of the paper she'll have my ass in a sling."

"So you came here to tell me the bet's off."

"Hell, no. I'm still going to win. I want a side deal."

"Ah, yes, which brought you to me at midnight. And that is?" She appeared wary but intrigued.

"The way I see it, we're chasing the same story, but neither of us has a clue what it is. Am I right so far?"

She paused, then nodded.

He began to pace, ticking off points against his fingers. "Cadman's supposedly building a wilderness retreat, but we don't know where or when. He's got to be involved in Bald is Beautiful. Why? He's getting his snooty rich friends involved, too. Again, why? Those people won't talk to me, but they will talk to you."

"Yes." She smiled sweetly. "They will talk to me."

He kept his gaze level as he stopped pacing and turned to her. "But I have all the background and research on Cadman. Interviews, sources in the construction business, gossip, lots of little goodies I can't confirm but could help us get to the bottom of this story."

"Such as?"

"Such as this Nathan Macarthur who owns that numbered company. Who is he? A front for Cadman?"

Her eyes blinked wide. "You found out who owns the numbered company?"

Oh, man, was she green. "Didn't they teach you how to do a numbered company search in journalism school?"

"Of course," she muttered, fussing with the drawstring at her neck. "I just ran out of time."

He held back his smirk and watched her face. "Name mean anything to you?"

"Nathan Macarthur?" She shook her head, slowly. "No."

"Damn." He'd been hoping she'd know. He was probably insane to pursue his deal with the rookie princess, but what other options did he have? He still believed her contacts would outweigh her lack of experience as his silent partner. He took a breath. "So?"

"So?" She crossed her arms under her breasts and he wished she wouldn't do that. It was like offering a starving man his favorite meal on a silver platter.

He forced himself to glance away. "So, I know Cadman had inside information on the bidding process on the opera house. I have so much dirt on that crook I need a backhoe to move my files. He's trying to pull another fast scam and this time I'm going to nail him. My deal is this—we share information. I'll give you access to all my research and files on Cadman. I've got sources it's taken me years to cultivate. You share all your notes and transcripts from interviews, anything you uncover that relates to this story."

She didn't say anything for a moment, and he knew she was working out the pros and cons in her head, as he had before approaching her.

He settled back to wait, knowing she'd agree if she was anywhere near the serious journalist she pretended to be. They worked together or gave up on the story. It was as simple as that.

"What about our bet?"

"The bet stands. This is only about sharing information."

"You mean—"

"Front-page story. The first to get one wins."

"But what if the Cadman story is our only chance at the front page?" She sounded a little nervous.

"We agree not to go public until we have a solid story."

She nodded.

"Then it's up to whichever one of us can sell the story to our editor first."

Her eyes widened. "You mean you'd scoop me?"

He grinned at her naiveté. "Scoop or be scooped, babe. That's how the game is played."

She let out her breath in a huff and he thought he'd lost her. Then she seemed to straighten her spine. "All right," she said slowly, her gaze caught by something across the room.

He followed the direction of her gaze to a silver-framed picture of her father. There was another of her mother beside it, but it was her father she stared at as she took up his challenge.

So she wanted to show dear old dad, did she? Interesting. An expression both vulnerable and sweet swept her face, giving him a rare glimpse beneath her cool facade. It made him want to cross the room and take her into his arms. Which scared him so much he put his half-empty long-neck down on her desk with a thunk. She was royalty and he was the poor slob who emptied the chamber pots of her world. He had to remember that.

"I'll be on my way, princess. Thanks for the beer."

"Wait." She jerked her attention from the picture and caught his gaze, her eyes luring him. "How will we share information? Obviously it would look suspicious if we start spending time together, when everybody knows..."

"Everybody knows what?"

"That...well, we don't exactly have a lot in common. Read my movie reviews sometime."

"Maybe everybody is wrong." He stepped closer, and, unable to stop himself indulging in a quick taste of her, tipping her chin and kissed her swiftly. "Anyhow, we see each other all the time at the movies." He pulled away to see her half-dreamy expression, her plump pink lips soft and parted, their cool beer-flavored imprint still burning his own. Uh-oh. Bad, bad mistake. The kiss had been an irresistible impulse, a way to seal their bargain, but now that he'd had a taste of her, he couldn't find the strength to pull away.

She made a small sound in her throat, part plea, part sigh, and he was lost. He pulled her to him. One hand went to the nape of her neck, to hold her in place. Her hair danced and played along his skin. Keeping his eyes on hers, he lowered his mouth slowly this time, brushing it back and forth against her lips while her eyes went soft. She sighed against him, her head tilting back against his supporting hand in a way that begged him to deepen the kiss.

He wasn't one to turn down an invitation like that. But still he didn't rush, enjoying her softness and surprise, watching her eyelids flutter shut and letting his own do the same as he trailed his tongue with careful deliberation around her parted lips. Then, he dipped inside, tasting, exploring—a deep, wet, intense kiss that tasted of cold beer and hot woman.

Her computer hummed quietly in the background. Somewhere outside a horn honked, but he heard only her quiet sighs and quickened breathing.

She felt warm and right in his arms, fitting as though they'd been molded for each other. Against his chest her breasts flattened and he knew he'd guessed right. There was nothing between them but sweatshirt. And that was far too much. He brought both hands to her waist and slowly raised the fleece until his fingertips skimmed creamy soft flesh that quivered at his touch. She didn't protest, in fact her hands clutched at his shoulders, silently urging him on. Higher he took his questing hands, until they climbed past her rib cage and reached the firm swell of her breasts.

As was everything else about Tess Elliot, her breasts were damn near perfect. Not too big, not too small, but tastefully just right.

It was his turn to moan as he filled his hands with her, the hard points teasing his palms. Still kissing her deeply, he kneaded the flesh, pinched the puckered nipples lightly so she gasped and clutched at him mindlessly. She returned his kiss with a fierceness that amazed him from someone who'd always appeared so calm and controlled. He'd misjudged her, he realized, the Ice Princess wasn't a melter—she was a volcano.

He opened his eyes to check his bearings, find the door to her bedroom. Even as he moved to lift her into his arms, she mumbled, "No. We have to stop."

"That is a terrible idea."

She pulled away from his mouth and rested her cheek against his chest. "Mmm, I know. But we're rivals."

"Right now, I'd say we're on the same team."

She chuckled softly, looking absurdly beautiful with her hair mussed, her lips soft and pouty and her cheeks flushed. "Tell you what. After I feed you crow, we'll see about—" she gazed up at him, her arm gesturing between them "—about this."

"First. *I'll* be cooking the crow. Second, you'll never be able to resist me that long."

Laughter danced in her eyes. "What's this? Another bet?"

He grinned back at her. "Don't waste your money. You haven't got a chance."

Then, pretending it didn't kill him to do so, he strode to the door and let himself out.

"SHOVE OVER."

"Pardon?" Tess glanced up and there was Mike, overflowing popcorn in one hand, a soda in the other, jerking his head for her to move over a seat. He acted as though he'd forgotten all about kissing her almost senseless, which, knowing Mike and his reputation, he probably had.

"I always sit on the aisle," she protested, feeling both cranky and insulted that he seemed well-rested when she'd barely slept the past few nights thinking about him...wanting him. She might not have a ton of experience with men, but she was pretty sure all that passion hadn't come from her. "You always sit across the aisle," she reminded him.

"We can't whisper secrets if we don't sit together," he said, his eyes burning with intent. Not lust, as her flip-flopping heart first thought, but suppressed knowledge.

"You know something?" She moved, her reporter instincts winning over her bruised feminine pride, and let him have the aisle seat.

"I know lots of things," he said in a tone that made her roll her eyes. "Popcorn?" He thrust the massive carton at her, causing three or four puffy white pieces to fall on her lap.

"No, thanks." She pushed it back. "Why does your popcorn always overflow?"

"Chick at the concession has a crush on me," he said, stuffing popcorn into his mouth. "She gives me extra."

"The teenager with the attitude? I suppose she can't help herself." The smell of popcorn made her mouth water. She shouldn't be hungry after a tofu stir-fry, but the junk-food aroma tantalized her.

"Did you talk to the Peabodys?" he asked around a mouthful of popcorn.

Did he think she was that naive? "Tell me your news first."

He drank from the yellow plastic straw, his eyes measuring her over the lid of the soda. Blue, blue eyes that gave a woman thoughts she shouldn't be having. "Cadman played golf yesterday."

"His doctor will be thrilled."

He waited her out, making her ask.

"All right. With whom did he play golf?"

His eyes crinkled. "*Whom* is an official of our fair city."

There was only one official who would get Mike this excited. "You mean, the mayor?"

He nodded.

She reached into his tub absently. "They've been friends for years. I think they were fraternity brothers." She pushed popcorn into her mouth, enjoying the burst of salt and butter flavors.

"The mayor—the same mayor who slipped Cadman a peek at the construction bids on the opera house—and another guy."

"You weren't able to prove your allegations about the mayor," she reminded him.

"Yeah. I know. But they're true all the same. And since then, they've hardly been seen together. That's what makes this so interesting."

"Who was the third man?"

He shook his head and scooped more popcorn, then tipped the carton her way and she helped herself. "Didn't recognize him. I don't think he's from around here. Fiftyish, balding, terrible golfer."

"That narrows it down." The lights in the theater dimmed and the first preview rolled onto the screen. She was thirsty and without thinking, leaned over and sucked the straw, buzzed by the sizzling sweetness as the cola hit her tongue.

"Want me to get you one?"

"Hmm?" She gasped as she realized she'd just drunk from Mike's straw. "I'm sorry. I wasn't paying attention."

"That's okay," he said. "Sharing's good." But his voice sounded a little husky, as though the popcorn had scratched his throat. He took the straw for a sip and lifted his gaze. His lips closed over the place where hers had just rested.

The gesture was as deliberate, as intimate as a kiss. Even as she watched him suck the liquid up through the straw, she felt her own mouth go dry. She licked her lips and felt a sizzle on her tongue that had nothing to do with carbonation.

With a start she turned toward the screen where cartoon images flashed and bounced. "Maybe he just felt like golfing," she whispered to Mike without daring to glance at him.

He shifted and his arm pressed against hers, as though they were on a real date. "Cadman never does anything just for fun. Golf games are always about business. He left town a couple of hours after the game."

A thought occurred to her and she turned to him, watched the light from the film flicker over his profile, making him seem mysterious and fascinating. "What were you doing at the golf course? I wouldn't have thought golf was your game."

"I've got a buddy who works there. He lets me know when Cadman plays."

"You spy on Mr. Cadman?"

"Just doing my job."

Job. Right. This was a job. Sitting beside Mike in the dim theater, so close they were touching it was hard to remember this was strictly business.

She glanced at the movie patrons in the rows ahead, couples mostly. She saw arms around shoulders, heads leaning close to each other, a quick kiss. She and Mike must look like those dating couples: sharing popcorn, a drink, going home together after the show to pick up where they'd left off…. *No. Bad idea.* This might feel like a date, but it was work.

"Did you take pictures?" she murmured.

A short pause. "I might have."

"Let me see them when they're developed. It's possible I'll recognize the person."

"I'll swing 'round to your place after I pick them up from the drugstore."

"Drugstore?" She turned to him once more. "Won't your photography department develop them?"

"Sure they would. And my ass would be fired within the hour."

She winced. "Sorry. I forgot." He had a lot riding on this story. So did she. They couldn't afford to make a mistake.

"Any luck finding out who Nathan Macarthur is?"

"Lives in Spokane. Has a couple of kids and a mortgage. He's owned the Pasqualie River property for at least twenty years. He doesn't work for Cadman, he sells insurance. How about you? Get in to see Margaret Peabody yet?"

Tess shook her head. "She's out of town, too. But I did drop by my mother's club and have lunch with her today."

"Well, that's a big help. My lunch took ten minutes and came with ketchup and mustard. Yours?"

"I left after two hours. I didn't even have time for the dessert trolley."

"Please. I'm gonna cry."

"Cry then. I won't bother telling you about my conversation with Mmes. Brewster, Spencer, Ellis and Lowe."

He glanced at her with scorn. "Pasqualie ladies who lunch. What did you talk about? New ways to keep your diamonds shiny?"

She smiled at him. An empty social smile. He did not deserve to be working with her. "The spring social calendar, actually."

A beat passed in his tiny reptilian brain. He must realize she'd brought up the subject for a reason. She simply stared at him until he gave in and asked, "Anything else?"

"Well, as a matter of fact, they all contributed to B.I.B."

She smoldered at him until he huffed. "Okay, you have different sources than me."

She really wanted to punish him, but she wanted to share more information. "Those women were all approached by a couple of new club members who sold them B.I.B. memberships to help save the eagles. They were younger women. I recognized one of the names. A friend of Jennifer Cadman's."

Oh, she had his attention now. "Cadman's daughter? Coincidence?"

"Not unless it's a coincidence that both members work for Mr. Cadman."

"I know Jennifer collects a paycheck from her dad. Supposedly, she does P.R. or something."

Tess nodded. "I asked my mother. The woman who sold memberships also work for him."

"What is his game?"

"I don't know," she said. "But we're going to find out."

TESS WAS CHOPPING vegetables for a dinner salad the next evening when her door buzzer rang. She seriously considered ignoring it, knowing who was at the door. Only one person in her life showed up without the courtesy of a phone call first. It buzzed again, sounding like a long irritable *hurry up.*

She popped a slice of red pepper into her mouth and crunched it while she made her way slowly to the intercom. Mike was pretty much impossible to ignore. Besides, she wanted to see those golf pictures.

"Hey, Tess." He breezed in once she'd let him up.

She was torn between pleasure at seeing him and annoyance at his casual assumption that she'd be alone and able to drop everything at his whim. "Does it ever occur to you I might be entertaining?"

He jumped back into the hall, his face registering ludicrous horror. "What, your high-society friends?"

"No! I don't have— I mean..." She sighed and opened the door wider. "Come in. As it happens there's no one here. What I'm trying to say is, I'd appreciate it if you'd call first."

He lowered his voice and his eyes twinkled, "Afraid I'll catch you in flagrante delicto?"

Her cheeks grew warm and she opened her mouth to tell him he most certainly would not find her in flagrante anything, then decided she didn't need to tell him about her private life. All they'd shared was a couple of steamy kisses, not enough to give him prying rights. She settled on an enigmatic, "Perhaps."

For a second his eyes flamed with dangerous heat. Jaw set, he stomped past her into the apartment once more, muttering.

"I beg your pardon?" She didn't know whether to be amused or irritated that it obviously hadn't occurred to him she might entertain male company—other than him.

"I'm saying we need to have some rules about this if we're working together. No..." He made a circular gesture with his hands, as a conductor would to the violin section.

"No...?" She made the gesture back to him, wondering what on earth he was trying to say.

"No flagrante delicto so long as we're working together."

"I didn't know celibacy was part of the deal." Exasperation crept into her tone; she was still irritated she'd let that kiss get so out of hand the other night. "Does that go for both of us?"

He turned to her, scowling. "My place is a worse rental dump than this. That's why your apartment is operation central. We keep all files, notes, photographs here. You let one of your high-society pretty boys in here, they might go squealing to Uncle Tyrone. Then our goose would be cooked but good."

"Your goose, actually," she reminded him. "My goose is nowhere near the fire."

He shot her a filthy look, then dug out a photo from the leather satchel slung over his shoulder. "You know this guy?"

The color eight-by-ten showed Ty Cadman with the mayor and another man in earnest conversation. They leaned on golf clubs, but something about the intensity in their expressions made Tess think they weren't talking about the next hole. As Mike had already told her, the man with Mr. Cadman was in his fifties, balding and it seemed to her he wore golf clothes as though they belonged to someone else. Mr. Cadman, on the other hand, appeared as relaxed as if he lived in his golf duds. "Interesting."

"So? Do you know him?"

She shook her head. "I've never seen him, although..." She racked her memory but couldn't come up with anything. "He looks vaguely familiar."

"My buddy said he's not a regular or a club member. Cadman booked the tee time and signed this guy in as a guest."

"Could he be another old school friend?"

He gestured to the photo. "Didn't look to me like they were talking about bogies and birdies."

"Hmm?" She raised her head from the photo, puzzled.

"Haven't you ever golfed?"

She shuddered and shook her head. Just the thought of those ladies' foursomes with cocktails to follow made her shy away from the sport.

"That's golf jargon. A birdie is when you hit one under par, a bogie means you shot one too many and an eagle is when—"

Her soft gasp stopped him.

"What?"

"Eagles." She rubbed the tip of her tingling nose. "That's why his face was familiar. I'm almost certain he was in a group photo in the B.I.B. office. That man is somehow involved in Bald is Beautiful."

"Come on, Cadman would cook an eagle and eat it before he'd try to save it."

Above her desk hung a bulletin board. Mike found a pushpin and stuck the photo on the board next to a reminder of her next dentist appointment.

Without so much as asking her permission, he pulled open her middle drawer and found a felt marker. "Who and why?" he scribbled across the top of the photo, his handwriting just as illegible as she'd guessed it would be.

"There has to be a connection with B.I.B." she said, wishing she had more than gut intuition to go on.

"What's an environmental group got to do with Cadman?" Mike asked.

"I don't know. But his employees are selling B.I.B. memberships."

"Could be coincidence." He slipped off his sneakers, then his navy socks and began to pace her living room. "But I think you're right. Bald is Beautiful is the key."

"We need a copy of that member list," Tess said, watching his bare feet track across the cheap carpet. He had sexy feet. Long and narrow, the toes straight and the nails square. A tiny tuft of black hair grew on the knuckle of each big toe.

"How do you feel about a little breaking and entering?"

She gaped at him. "Are you determined to end up in jail?"

"All for a good cause."

"You'd also get fired," she reminded him, knowing he dreaded that more than a jail cell.

"There is that." He went back to pacing, a frown of concentration on his face. Then suddenly he stopped. "We'll have to infiltrate the organization."

What was wrong with the man? "Mike! We're reporters not the FBI."

He didn't seem to hear her. He continued pacing. "Did you join B.I.B.?"

"Yes, but that was because—"

"I'll join, too. We'll go to the meetings, maybe get you elected to the board or something. Even a crackpot bunch of bird lovers must have a board of some kind. No, dammit. That will take forever." He snapped his fingers. "Secretary. Volunteer to be their secretary. Then you can have access to all their records."

"Isn't that kind of obvious?"

He shrugged. "You're right. Stealing's better."

She huffed out a breath. "While you plan a life of crime, I'll get back to making dinner."

That caught his attention. "Sounds good. What are we having?"

"*I* am having salad."

He followed her to the kitchenette and leaned against the single bank of cupboards while she went back to chopping. "That's an awful lot of salad for one person," he said, snagging a snow pea.

He was incredibly cute when he wheedled, plus she

felt that a brainstorming session might be exactly what they needed. "You can stay if you do the dishes."

"Great. Do you have any steak or anything to go with all that green stuff?"

She raised her eyebrows, gave him a don't-push-it look and went back to chopping.

"No. Really. You need some more meat on your bones."

She sighed. Wheedling and begging—how could they be so endearing? "I've got some free-range chicken breasts."

"Do you have cornmeal?"

"Pardon?"

But he was already opening her cupboards. "Cornbread." He pawed through packets and jars and she heard a groan. "Does everything in your kitchen have to be organic?"

"Yes."

"Do you have any *organic* cornmeal?"

"No."

"Ah, flour. No time for yeast. Scones. Do you have cheese?"

His muttering amused her. Did he really think she was going to make him scones? She didn't even think she had a recipe. She started to answer, but he was already in her fridge pulling out cheese and eggs.

"I'm not cooking you scones," she said.

"*I'm* cooking *you* scones."

And, much to her surprise, he started, showing a skill and comfort in the kitchen that amazed her.

As she continued with the salad, he rolled up his sleeves, washed his hands and went to work. He leaned around her to turn on the stove and his arm brushed hers. She couldn't prevent the shiver of awareness as her body felt his heat and her nostrils recognized his scent.

For a long moment he didn't move but stayed behind her, rigid, his breath stirring the hair on the back of her neck so it felt like a caress. She waited, instinctively sensing the tension within him, wondering if it would crack and he'd drag her into his arms. Wondering what she'd do if he tried.

He hadn't in any way acknowledged the passion that had flared between them, and even though it had kept her awake at night, she refused to broach the subject. But she wasn't a convenient body whenever he felt like a little extracurricular nooky; she hoped she'd have the strength to prove it by rejecting his advances.

Her heart rate picked up and she licked her lips, but her resolve wasn't put to the test.

He retreated to his eggs and mixing bowl. "While you suck up to the bird people, I'm going to take a drive to Spokane."

All thoughts of kissing fled as she turned to stare at him. She was a rule follower, and to her mind stalking a man merely because he'd played golf with Mr. Cadman was bending the rules to breaking point. "Mike, you're not—"

"Yep. I'm going to visit Mr. Nathan Macarthur. I think I'll buy some insurance."

While the scones were baking, he grilled the chicken breast in her toaster oven, then delved back into her cupboards and pulled out the walnut oil she'd bought for something or other. "Do you have any wine vinegar?"

She gave up being shocked, or insulted, that he'd taken an invitation to dinner as a chance to play guest chef in her kitchen. "Cupboard above the fridge."

When they sat down to dinner with fresh steaming scones and a chicken dish that looked as if it came straight out of a gourmet cooking magazine, she decided to let it go. When she bit into the flaky scone she almost moaned with pleasure and forgave him completely. "When did you learn to cook?"

"When I figured out it was the fastest way to get a woman into bed."

She chuckled. "I thought your charm alone would do the trick."

He shook his head sadly. "Women are tougher than you think." He shot her a teasing glance, but something hot sizzled beneath it, making her stomach curl. "Look how long we've been seeing each other. Haven't had you falling into bed with me."

There was a pause while the temperature in the room seemed to rise. She finally managed to speak, but her voice wasn't her own. "Don't think a few scones are going to do the trick."

He laughed and helped himself to more salad, breaking the moment. But she had to wonder, if he put his mind to seducing her, how long she'd hold out. After the way they'd behaved the other night, she wouldn't put money on her own chances of remaining unseduced. And the scones, delicious chicken and salad dressing had nothing to do with her weakness for him. She took another bite of scone, flaky and warm, the butter she'd spread just melting— Well, they didn't have much to do with it.

To change the subject, and her train of thought, she said, "Margaret Peabody's back in town. We're meeting tomorrow."

"Great," he said around a mouthful of chicken, "I'll come with you."

"No, you won't. Are you crazy? She already reported you to your boss."

He shook his head. "Wasn't Margaret. That was her not-so-better half. Look, Tess. No offense, but you don't know how to do an interview. You've got no experience at this kind of thing. You have to read body language, delve beyond the obvious, ask the tough questions. Listen to what's not being said."

"Thanks for the lesson," she said with frigid politeness. "And once again, no. You can't come."

"This is my story, too. I'm willing to go to jail for it. You can invite me to tea, can't you?"

She shrugged. "We're meeting at Café Trieste for coffee. You can sit at a nearby table and watch her body language."

He made a face. "Café Trieste? That's that grotesque yuppie place where your kind hangs out."

"You got it."

"I'm not—"

She raised her hand. "That's as big a concession as you're getting. And if you try anything smart, the whole deal is off."

"All right." He groaned. "Café Trieste, where coffee has forty-seven names, costs nine bucks, and none of it tastes like coffee."

"So stay home."

He scowled at her. "What time tomorrow?"

6

Kick It *made me wish the P.I. heroine would kick the sexy-but-dim-witted police officer hero out of every scene but the bedroom ones.*

TESS ARRIVED at the coffee shop ten minutes early, wanting to be certain of securing seats. She was lucky enough to nab one of the prize window tables since she arrived just as a couple was leaving. The woman was speaking into a cell phone, the man checking e-mail on his Blackberry.

Mike was going to hate it here, she thought smugly as she pulled a notebook out of her bag, thinking she'd work while she waited. She shoved it in again. No reason to remind Margaret Peabody she was a reporter. Instead, she ordered a cappuccino and dug into her bag once more, this time for the *Wall Street Journal*.

The pages rustled importantly, but she didn't read. She mentally rehearsed the things she wanted to find out from her mother's friend. She felt a little guilty using the family connection as a ruse to gain information, but, she reasoned, she was a reporter. She had to toughen up. Besides, Margaret Peabody wouldn't be hurt. It was Ty Cadman Tess and Mike were after.

Giving up on an article about the national economy, she sat back and simply enjoyed her coffee. She loved this place. It smelled of espresso and chocolate, steamed milk and biscotti, while the constant shush and spurt of the coffee bar sounded like a steam engine chugging through the Italian Alps.

Café Trieste was owned by a Tuscan family and the coffee jockeys called out their instructions in Italian. The walls were burnt umber, the floor terra-cotta tile, and the china hand-painted with stylized flowers on twining green stems. It hardly took any imagination at all to transport herself to the Tuscan hills.

She smiled at the idea of really being there. If she saved diligently maybe she could take a trip to Italy next summer. Of course, she could dip into her trust fund—there was nothing her grandmother would love more than for Tess to return to Europe—but it had become almost an obsession to live her life on her own terms and to manage on her salary.

She licked foam from her lip. Perhaps she was taking pride a bit far, but everything was sweeter when she earned it herself. Besides, she did manage to save money. She could afford a European vacation. Not at five-star hotels, but if she bought a rail pass, kept her eye out for cheap air tickets and found budget accommodation, she could squeak out a couple of weeks in Italy.

Excitement began to build. She'd visit Rome and wander around pretending she was Audrey Hepburn in *Roman Holiday*. Of course she'd have no Gregory Peck. She leaned back in her chair. He'd been a reporter in that movie. Audrey'd been a…a princess.

All at once she imagined herself and Mike in Rome, but she envisioned not the Colosseum or the Trevi Fountain, not the Sistine Chapel or the catacombs. What came to mind was a cozy double bed with white cotton sheets in a simple room with shutters. And what she saw happening on that bed made her heart thump.

As though her erotic fantasy had conjured him, Mike strode through the door, black hair loose around his shoulders, black jacket open to the waist, black helmet hanging from his fingers. He scanned the room, caught sight of her and winked.

The wide cup rattled as she hastily set it down. If he could read her thoughts...

He made no other sign of recognition, but approached the coffee bar. She held back a smile when the young man handed him a mug painted with flowers. He rolled his eyes and took himself off to the long wooden counter with stools that gave him a good view of her table.

Back to the *Wall Street Journal* and the nation's finances. She felt his presence, felt his gaze on her, even as she tried once again to concentrate. Two full readings of the article and she still didn't have a clue whether the gross domestic product was in good shape or bad.

"Here I am, Tess. I hope I'm not late." Margaret Peabody's voice couldn't have come at a more welcome time.

"No. You're not late. It's nice to see you." Tess smiled as she folded the paper and rose to air kiss her mother's friend. For as long as she could remember, Margaret Peabody had smelled of Chanel No. 5—she used the soap, the body powder and the perfume.

But today she smelled like a new woman. Something exotic and spicy.

"You changed your perfume," Tess said before she could stop herself.

Mrs. Peabody didn't seem offended by the personal comment. She beamed. "Yes. I needed a change."

Only now, when Tess pulled away, did she note that perfume wasn't all that was different. The woman's hair was blond and cut into a stylish, tousled crop that made her look years younger. She wore a scoop-necked blouse, a leather skirt and knee-length leather boots. "You look great." Tess said weakly, wondering what had happened to the real Margaret Peabody, the one who looked old enough to be Harrison's mother. "Can I get you a coffee?"

"Just herbal tea, thanks. Perhaps something with ginger in it."

"The almond croissants are fantastic." She knew Mrs. Peabody's sweet tooth and had sought to butter her up, quite literally.

The blond head shook. "I'm dieting," she whispered.

Returning a few minutes later with a second cappuccino for herself and the herbal tea, she caught Mike staring at her guest. The woman didn't look a bit like the middle-aged rather frumpy woman of Tess's description, which wouldn't improve his opinion of her observational powers.

She set the drinks on the round table and decided to start right in on the excuse she'd come up with for this meeting. "I'm stumped. Mother's birthday is in a few weeks and I haven't got a clue what to get her. I was hoping you might have some ideas."

"Oh, goodness. It is difficult, isn't it? The woman has everything." Mrs. Peabody sipped her tea, then set her cup down.

Since Tess already had her mother's gift—a Victorian scarf pin with garnets and seed pearls that she knew her mom would love—she let her guest ramble on.

"Her garden's lovely, and you know how she prizes her roses, but I don't think there's room for a single new stem."

"No. The gardener's already threatening to dig up the older roses." She glanced up, feeling Mike's gaze burn into her, warm and distracting.

"She loves Victorian trinkets. You might try an antique shop."

"Oh." She loosened her collar, feeling suddenly warm. "What a great idea! Thanks."

"Or it's always nice to make a donation to a charity in the person's name. Especially when it's for someone who has everything."

Tess could have kissed Mrs. Peabody. Keeping her voice casual she said, "That's a fantastic idea. Is there a particular charity—or cause—you like to support?"

"Oh, indeed." She nodded firmly.

Yes, yes, yes! Tess waited for a mention of eagles and B.I.B.

"My women's group raises money to help educate young girls in Third World countries." She shook her newly blond head sadly. "I think your mother already donated quite heavily this year."

"That's a wonderful cause," Tess agreed, but not the one she wanted to talk about at the moment. She ran her index finger around the lip of her coffee cup as she gazed intently at the other woman. "I recently joined an environmental organization called Bald is Beautiful."

"Really? I think we support that one, too."

Tess's pulse kicked up as she worked on keeping

her face and voice calm. "You do? What a coincidence."

"Someone recommended it, I can't remember who. One of the young people at the club. It might have been Jennifer Cadman."

Ty Cadman's daughter. She glanced at Mike again, as though for inspiration, but of course he wasn't close enough to hear.

They chatted a bit about mutual acquaintances and how Harrison was enjoying his job in his father's bank. "Harrison invited me to the opening of the new opera center, you know. We had a very nice time. Mr. Cadman stopped and chatted for a few minutes."

She watched over the rim of her cup. Was it her imagination? Did Mrs. Peabody twitch a bit at the mention of Ty Cadman. "Did he? I found the leads a little weak, but the costumes were lovely."

No, no, no! Tess didn't want to talk about singers and costumes. She wanted dirt on Cadman. She tried again. "Isn't the building gorgeous?"

"Oh my, yes. Difficult to be tasteful with so much marble, but I think Ty managed it nicely."

Beneath the table Tess crossed her fingers. "I wonder what he'll work on next?"

"He's always busy. I believe he's working on a casino, a hotel and he mentioned something about a planned community he's involved with."

Tess's eyes almost bugged out at the unexpected news. "A casino? And a planned community? What, here?"

"Oh, not the planned community. No." Margaret Peabody shrugged her recently slimmer shoulders. "Ty helped us buy some land as an investment somewhere near the city. He says it will increase in value because of the hotel and casino project. He's always been good like that, passing on tips. Of course, it's all hush-hush at the moment."

"Oh, naturally." She smiled. "That sounds interesting. Why does he think the land will rise in value?"

"Pardon?" Margaret Peabody frowned slightly. Of course, this wasn't exactly typical coffee chat for women such as them.

Tess waved the *Wall Street Journal,* delighted she'd brought it with her. "I have to start thinking of my own financial future. I was reading about the state of the economy before you arrived." She swallowed, hoping Margaret Peabody hadn't added an interest in national finance to her new hobbies. "Who knows what the future holds?"

"Perhaps you should talk to Ty. I know he has quite a bit of land. He's putting together a syndicate to develop a hotel complex. It's on the river so there will be fishing and nature activities."

"And, I believe you mentioned a casino."

"Yes. I don't care for gambling myself, but people seem to like it."

Tess's mind was racing. Could he possibly be planning to put a casino in a wildlife refuge? She sipped her coffee absently, and found it had gone cold.

She smiled at her companion. "You've been a great help," she said. "I think I'll hit the antique shops this afternoon and find something for Mother."

"My pleasure, Tess. Thank you for the tea. I've got to run now. I've got an appointment with my personal trainer."

They rose and air kissed once more. After which Tess stood rooted to the spot staring after the swishing, leather-clad hips of a woman older than her

mother. A woman who used to look like her grandmother and could now pass for her sister. *Personal
trainer?*

"You didn't tell me your mom's friend was a hottie," came a deep voice from behind her.

"She wasn't last time I saw her," Tess replied, stuffing her newspaper back into her bag and gathering
her things to leave.

Mike waited for her. "I'll walk you out."

"How polite."

He snorted. "Cough up the goods." He opened the
door and she passed through.

Cough up the goods, indeed. She decided to tease
him a little first. "Well, my mother's birthday is coming up. Mrs. Peabody had some excellent sugg—"

"Dammit, there's Mel." Suddenly, Mike grabbed
her hand. She was so astonished she turned to gape at
him. He tried to drag her back into the coffee shop but
an older Italian gentleman was coming out. *"Mi
scusi,"* he said, edging around them and then Mike's
managing editor was in front of them, staring at their
clasped hands.

"Hiya Mel," Mike boomed in a overly cheerful
voice.

"What's going on?" The woman stopped dead in
her tracks and glared from Mike to Tess and back
again.

Tess had seen Mel a few times but never had been
introduced. The woman had a fearsome reputation for
ruling her small newspaper kingdom by fear. Hearing
the gravelly voice and noting the way her gaze
speared them, Tess could believe it.

She tried to tug her hand free, but Mike held it in a
grip so tight she feared her bones were bending. He

continued in the same falsely jovial tone. "Mel, do you know Tess Elliot?"

Mel sent her a curt nod. "I know your father."

So what else was new? Would she ever be acknowledged for her own work? She wanted to be known as Tess Elliot the journalist, not Tess, the daughter of Walt Elliot. She stopped tugging. This story was her best chance at making that happen. If holding hands with Mike Grundel was part of the price she had to pay, so be it.

"I'm a journalist with the Pasqualie *Standard*," she replied coolly.

"Sure you are, sweetie," Mel replied. "Those society columns keep me on the edge of my seat."

A few months ago Tess would have gasped at such rudeness. But she'd toughened up enough to know that Mel was baiting her. Instead of spluttering with indignation, she smiled. "You have to start somewhere."

To her surprise, the woman laughed—a smoker's wheeze that ended on a hacking cough. "Your movie reviews aren't half-bad. They need a good edit, all that highfalutin fluff hacked out. But there's hope."

Tess mumbled something unintelligible, which pretty much reflected the jumbled thoughts in her brain. The worst of it was, she felt flattered. This terrifying woman read her stuff—and saw promise. Tess determined to take a hard look at her next review before she turned it in. Fluff, huh?

"Yep. Too much fluff," Mike chimed in. "That's exactly what I tell her. Don't I, hon?"

"Hon?" Both Mel and Tess turned on him at the same time, repeating the revolting term.

He looked harassed. And desperate. "Yeah. We're

an item." Releasing Tess's hand, he threw an arm around her shoulders.

He squeezed her shoulder in warning, and she tried not to wince at the pain.

"Right," she agreed, nodding like one of those bouncy birds she'd seen in the back windows of cars. "An item."

Mel stared at Mike. "You told me she was a no-talent debutante and it was a punishment to have to review the same movies."

Tess felt her cheeks burn and tried to jerk away. "How dare—"

"That was then," Mike said, a manic edge to his tone. "This is now."

"Oh, no, you—" He shut her up by slapping his mouth over hers.

Thrown off balance she tumbled against his solid chest and, before she had time to go for her pepper spray, his mouth gentled and her mind fogged.

Even though she was rigid with anger she was still conscious of the heat and firmness of his lips and the dazzling electricity that surged between them.

For a moment she forgot where she was, whom she was kissing, and leaned into all that potent sexiness, clutching his muscular shoulders for support since her knees seemed to have melted out from under her.

He tasted like adventure, danger and glamour. And a bit like coffee. She smelled the leather of his coat, the all-male scent coming off his skin, and the faint whiff of cigarette smoke.

It was the cigarette smoke that brought her to her senses. *Mel.* Right, this was a charade for Mel's benefit. She pulled away from his lips, but they followed her until, with a reluctant jerk, she broke the kiss.

Still, she gazed into his eyes, smoky-blue and hot with desire. She felt an answering tug deep in her belly.

"Well." The gravelly voice brought them back to reality with a start. "I thought you were making it up. I guess opposites do attract, but I never would have believed you two were lovers if I hadn't seen it with my own eyes. Mike Grundel and Tess Elliot." The idea seemed to amuse her, and she stalked past them into the café chuckling.

"Oh, my God. What have I done?" Mike's forehead creased and he took a step after her. "Wait, Mel. It's not what you think, we're not— Ow." He glared down at Tess. "What did you kick me for."

"For being a bonehead. You've just convinced her we're an item. Don't make her change her mind."

"But she'll tell everybody at the *Star*. They'll laugh themselves sick. I've gotta go and stop her. Ow!" He jumped back and bent to rub his shin.

"You are such a jerk. Stay away from me," she said, and stomped off down the sidewalk, shoulder bag swinging angrily at her side.

He caught up with her at the curb, grasping her upper arm. "You promised to tell me what Margaret Peabody said."

"You're the expert on body language. You figure it out." The walk light blinked and she stepped off the curb and strode ahead, staring at the opposite curb.

"What are you so steamed about?"

She stopped dead in the center of the intersection. "I'll make this easy for you. Body language basics." She flipped him the bird.

She kept walking and for several seconds she had the road to herself.

She gained the other side and continued down the sidewalk before he appeared once more at her side. "I can't believe you did that—that obscene gesture. What if Mel saw you?"

"She'd be able to tell your colleagues what I really think of you and they wouldn't laugh themselves sick thinking you and I were dating."

This time he stopped her bodily, pulling her over to the side of a building and turning her to face him. "Hey, is that what's got you so riled? I didn't mean it like that." His blue eyes scanned her face, pausing at her lips for long enough that she had to fight the urge to run her tongue across them to cool the heat. "Come on. If a story got out about us, your people would yank your chain, too."

Her eyes widened as the truth sunk in. She imagined the ribbing she'd take from Steve in sports, the guys in photography—even Caro and Jonathon would relish the joke.

But still, he'd been more eager to convince Mel they *weren't* an item than that they were. "You're sure it's not me?"

He looked genuinely shocked. "No. Of course it's not you. Most guys would give their left, uh, arm to go out with you."

She snorted. "Yes. They're lining up for the chance."

"If they're not it's because you scare them. You're so...I don't know. Cool and unattainable."

Cool and *unattainable* were not words that gave her sexual confidence a power surge. Moments ago she'd kissed this man on a public street. That didn't seem very cool or unattainable. An interesting thought occurred to her. "Do I scare *you?*"

He reached out and tucked her hair behind her ear. "You scare the hell out of me."

"Then why did you kiss me?"

He squinted at something over her shoulder. "I'm a boxer. I feinted her out. But I didn't think she'd believe us."

She remembered the passion of their embrace. Anybody would have believed there was something between them. She'd have believed it herself if she'd seen it.

Her gaze strayed to the scar on his lower lip.

"Tess?" His voice dropped to a sexy, husky whisper.

Instinct told her that if she stayed where she was, with her back against the window of Bert's Hardware, she was going to get another chance to feel the scar.

Part of her wanted to lean forward to meet him halfway. The sensible part put two and two together. The man didn't want their names linked, but he'd settle for public necking on Main Street on a Saturday morning. *Oh, no.*

She stopped him from kissing her the quickest way she knew how. "Margaret Peabody told me Ty Cadman helped them buy property as an investment. Apparently, the property's going to go up in value when it's developed into a casino and hotel complex."

When she'd started speaking he'd pulled away, a puzzled frown tugging his brows together. Presumably, women didn't usually step back from kissing him. Why was she not surprised? But, as her words sank in, puzzlement turned to excitement.

"He wants to put a gambling joint in an eagle sanctuary? I knew the bastard was up to something, but I never dreamed it could be this good. This time we nail him."

"We shouldn't jump to conclusions," she cautioned, even as her own stomach tied itself into knots. She rubbed her tingling nose absently. "The land Mrs. Peabody was talking about could be anywhere. Maybe she owns several pieces of land."

"Let's assume—" He glanced sharply over his shoulder as a passerby knocked into him with a brief word of apology. "We can't talk here. I'll meet you at your place later."

"When?"

He shrugged. "I don't know. Tonight sometime."

"Mike. It's Saturday."

"Oh, right." His gaze skimmed her face. "You got a hot date?"

"I'm going to a charity gala. As a matter of fact—"

"I predict another riveting story for the society page," he interrupted, a teasing light dawning in his eyes.

She narrowed her own gaze, having taken enough heat about her society stories for one day. "This is fair warning. The next kick won't be aimed at your shin."

He sucked in a breath. "Tell you what. Since you like fighting so much, come by the boxing club this afternoon and watch me pound your boss, Jon, into mush. We can talk there."

"Oh, yes. That's what I want to do with my free time. Sit in some old boys' club and breathe eau de testosterone." Still, at this point she'd do almost anything to move from the society page. Somehow, someday, there'd be a Pulitzer with her name on it. She wouldn't get there if she didn't occasionally do something she hated. Such as spend an afternoon with a bunch of troglodytes in some dank boxing club.

TESS WRINKLED HER NOSE as she stepped inside the Pasqualie Men's Pugilist Club.

In spite of the fancy name, as she'd feared, it stank. It smelled like half a century of sweat, dirty socks, spilled beer, dust and things she preferred not to contemplate.

Light came from harsh fluorescents mounted in the rafters. The highlights of the cavernous club seemed to be a single boxing ring, an area with exercise mats and four punching bags—two currently having the stuffing slugged out of them—and the corner closest to her with a bar/restaurant that looked as though it kept colonies of cockroaches in good health.

She shuddered and tried not to touch anything. When she'd agreed to meet Mike here, she'd had no idea it would be this bad. How could he stand this place?

How could Jonathon Kushner?

She didn't think she could spend another second here. She'd leave him a phone message, changing their meeting until tomorrow.

But as she turned to the exit, which promised fresh air and sunlight, Mike emerged from a doorway that presumably led to a change room. He wore a disreputable pair of gray shorts, a white tank top, fat red boxing gloves and a helmet.

He didn't see her, and she remained still, watching. He jumped nimbly up into the boxing ring and began to dance around, presumably to loosen up.

She forgot about fresh air and collapsed into the closest chair.

The man was built. Bronzed, muscular shoulders, flat stomach, strong legs.

Then he turned and she discovered his back view was just as enticing as the front.

"Okay, Jon. Knock me down. You know you want to." His voice echoed oddly as he taunted a second figure already in the ring. One she'd only just noticed. She had to admit, her friend's husband wasn't too bad, either. What was Jonathon Kushner doing here? He was as far out of his milieu as she. Intrigued, she decided to hang around to watch the former street kid and the millionaire fight it out.

She moved closer, but the two males circling in the ring were too absorbed in each other to notice her.

"All right. Touch your gloves, and I want a clean fight," grated the voice of an old man who stood in the center of the ring. Then he glared from one to the other of the bobbing and weaving opponents. "From both of yez."

They bumped gloves and backed off and the referee or whatever he was jumped back down to ground level to watch the action.

She saw Mike's and Jon's heads lower and two pairs of legs—one dark and muscular, one paler and more rangy—begin to bounce. She heard the thump of leather gloves against flesh, watched the men dance 'round each other, looking like fierce opponents rather than fast friends, and she moved closer still, fascinated.

The old man cast a glance her way as she stood beside him. His red-rimmed eyes narrowed. "I don't do no lady boxing. You want the pink joint down the street. *Tae bo.*" He used the maximum number of facial muscles to utter the last two words, letting her know how he felt about newfangled foreign concepts, then jerked his head toward the door and turned his attention back to the ring.

She was momentarily nonplussed. Was he throwing her out? Because of her gender? Not only was this behavior rude and politically incorrect, it was probably illegal to refuse women entry. As if she'd choose to be in this smelly old pit.

"I'm not interested in boxing myself. I simply want to watch the match. Those men are...friends of mine."

The old man snorted and rubbed a gnarled hand over his gray-stubbled chin. "These two been beating the crap out of each other—pardon my French—since they were kids." The rheumy eyes blinked. "Never knocked any sense into either of them."

Thump. Thumpthumpthumpthump. She didn't want to look, but she couldn't help herself.

"Come on, spit the silver spoon out of your mouth, buddy. Come and get it," Mike taunted.

He danced away and the Jon followed, fiercely focused, fists flying.

"Ow," Mike yelled. "I think he broke a rib."

"Shouldn'a teased him," said the old man. Tess glanced over and could have sworn he grinned, one swift twist of the lips and then it was gone. "Nice right hook."

She watched the rest of the match, or whatever this was, fascinated as they taunted and poked at each other like kids, both clearly enjoying a holiday from civilized adulthood. Well, Jon anyway. She wasn't certain Mike had ever attained civilized or adulthood.

"Come on, Mikey, scared I'll bite?"

After a bit she stopped flinching at every hit and just watched.

"Mike's good, isn't he?" she asked the old man.

"Yeah. He's been hanging around here since he was a delinquent himself. Now he coaches...whadya call 'em? Problem teens. After they get knocked on their asses—pardon my French—a few times, they don't make so many problems."

She watched until the old man called it over and they both jumped out of the ring and approached him. Only then did Mike seem to become aware of Tess. His stride hitched then he continued moving toward her. "Hey, Tess," he said casually.

"Hey, Mike." She tried to keep the smile off her face but couldn't quite manage it. Even though he was slick with sweat, she really wanted to hug him, not just for coaching troubled boys, but for being the best-camouflaged good guy she'd ever seen. Ty Cadman loved to parade his financial donations to charity, but she thought Mike—hiding behind his bad-boy clothes and attitude, but giving of his time and skill—was the truly generous one.

"Why, Tess. How nice to see you," Jonathon said, appearing beside Mike. He was too well brought up to show his curiosity, but she felt it all the same as he held out his gloves to the old man, who swiftly untied them.

"Hi, Jon." She wasn't going to make up some lame excuse about why she was here. She'd leave that for Mike.

He thrust his own gloves toward Tess. "Untie me?"

"Oh, sure." It felt strangely intimate somehow, but she managed without fumbling too badly, feeling Mike's gaze on her face the entire time, his breath evening slowly. A drop of sweat hit the gloves and bounced and she smelled the healthy perspiration from his workout.

She felt Jon's gaze on the pair of them and wished Mike would drop some glib explanation, but he didn't. The silence started to feel strained, and Jon, who was always smooth, headed for the change room with a brief wave.

By the time she got Mike's gloves off, Jon had already disappeared. "I never should have come here. I don't want Jon thinking we're chasing a hard news story any more than you wanted Mel to know."

"Don't worry about it. Jon's cool."

"Oh, good. What did you tell him?"

"That you're crazy about me and follow me everywhere with your tongue hanging out of your mouth."

Before she could come up with words that would blister him sufficiently, Mike turned to her, only barely keeping the grin in check. "Give me five minutes to shower and change. I'll be right out."

SHE MADE HER WAY to the gym's small cafeteria/bar and settled in the chair that looked the least grubby. She pulled it back a little from the table; calling *that* grubby would be a rare compliment.

While she steamed and thought up every devastating insult she could, Jon jogged by, hair soaking. "Nice seeing you, Tess," he said.

"Mike and I aren't..." Aren't what? She couldn't explain to her ultimate boss that she was working on an unauthorized news story, but she couldn't let him believe she was a Mike Grundel groupie, either. "We aren't serious," she choked out, her own fists clenched. She was going to hurt him when he emerged from his shower, and he'd need more than a helmet and fat gloves to protect him.

Jon sent her a grin that only upped her frustration. "Too bad for him. I've got to go. Caro's dragging me out shopping. I'm already late." And he was gone.

The outside door had barely closed when Mike appeared, hair hanging around his face in damp hanks, wearing a clean white T-shirt and jeans.

"Tell me again what Margaret Peabody said. Everything," he ordered as he flopped into the chair opposite hers while sucking on a water bottle.

"There's something I have to do first."

"What?"

"Kill you. How could you tell Jon I had a crush on you?"

His brows rose and a totally unrepentant twinkle appeared in his eyes. "Now you know how I felt in front of Mel this morning. I know it sucks, but pretending we're an item is our best chance to get away with working together."

"Well, just so you know, I'm dumping you first chance I get."

He chuckled. "We'll have to see about that. Come on, spill."

So she told him what her mother's friend had imparted over herbal tea.

"I thought about it all day," she said, "but the only explanation I can come up with is that Cadman's planning to develop a casino/hotel complex in the bird sanctuary. But why? Apart from the obvious zoning issues, and the desecration of sensitive habitat, why would he want to put a place like that out in the boonies?"

He shrugged. "He's going to need a huge piece of

land and if he wants riverfront, well, there isn't anything big close to town. The numbered company owns a good-size chunk right on the river. And I checked. There's no official environmental designation to stop it being developed. If Cadman can buy it from this Macarthur guy and keep the lid on the B.I.B. people, and get the mayor to push through a zoning change, it's a done deal."

She nodded, having come to the same conclusions. "He's got some pretty big hurdles to jump. But maybe we're wrong. Remember at the opera opening, Harrison Peabody referred to it as a wilderness retreat."

Mike snorted his derision. "Guy drives twenty miles thinks he's in the wilderness. Then he goes fishing and sends his wife to the casino."

"A wilderness casino. Interesting concept." She leaned forward, resting her chin on her laced fingers, then felt sticky goo under her elbows and withdrew them in disgust. "Mike, didn't you get the feeling, when you talked to Jeremy at Bald is Beautiful, that they act as if they own that land? Even though they obviously don't. Jeremy implied the owner was a friend of B.I.B."

Mike rose. "You want a Coke or something?"

"No, thank you."

He helped himself to a can from the refrigerator, dug out his wallet and put some money in a battered coffee tin. He popped the top and drank deeply before resuming his seat across from Tess. "If Macarthur is a friend of B.I.B.'s then Cadman's got something on him. He's using it to squeeze him off the land."

"Are you sure?"

"No, I'm guessing." He stretched his legs out in front of him and tipped his head back to contemplate the ceiling. She didn't follow suit. Likely there were bats up there.

"Zoning's Cadman's second problem. That land's not protected, but it's not zoned for commercial development either."

Mike nodded. "He's greased those wheels before." His face clouded and she knew he was recalling the story of municipal corruption he'd yet to prove. "Dammit, Tess. We've got to get him. I'll do some digging, pull all my files and we'll start putting together what we know. Let's say tomorrow night at your place for Operation Get Cadman. I'll bring dinner."

She nodded. "All right. I have to go. I'm covering the Rotary Club's big gala tonight. It's black tie." She glanced up at him with the most innocent expression she could manage. "Since we're an item now, maybe you should accompany me. As my date."

He choked on his cola. "Sorry, princess. I returned the monkey suit."

"Some other time, perhaps," she said, rising, feeling as though she'd got the last word for once.

She should have known better.

"Hey, princess?"

She paused, one hand on the door that led outside, to the **real** world. "Yes?"

"I told Jon I was nuts about you, too."

7

Since the caveman first threw a mastodon steak on the grill, man has enticed woman into the sack with food.

TESS ROLLED her shoulders to get some of the tightness out of them. "I wish you'd sit down, you're getting ketchup on the carpet."

Mike had shown up, as arranged. He'd brought dinner, as promised—take-out burgers and fries.

Her complaint didn't make a bit of difference. Mike kept pacing as though he hadn't heard her, stuffing another ketchup-soaked fry into his mouth.

"You might at least share." She'd already finished her fries.

"I drove to Spokane today."

"That's a pretty long Sunday drive."

He turned and kept pacing. "I felt like a nice long drive."

"Did you buy some insurance?"

"Didn't have to." He shot her a pleased grin. "I recognized the guy right away." Stopping in front of her bulletin board, he pointed to the picture of the golfing trip and tapped his finger over the unidentified golfer's face.

"Nathan Macarthur was the third man golfing with Cadman and the mayor? Great sleuthing partner." She wasn't really surprised, but this was the first evidence—circumstantial as it was—that linked Cadman with land along Pasqualie River.

Mike nodded. "He goes by Nate."

"You spoke to him?"

"Nope. He and the family pulled up not long after I got there, all decked out in their Sunday church best. I recognized him from the picture. His wife called him Nate."

Tess rolled her neck one more time. "So, we've got Macarthur, who's supposed to be a B.I.B. ally, doing business with Cadman."

"What the hell is Cadman planning? And why is there land in Margaret Peabody's name, and a bunch of other country club types, but not in Cadman's? Why, Tess, why?"

She gaped at him. He'd actually used her name. He hadn't called her princess. A little smile of satisfaction curled her lips. On his next pass, she snatched a fry out of the cardboard container. Chomping down, she grimaced. He'd not only slathered the things in ketchup, he'd doused them in vinegar, too. The man had no idea of subtlety. In anything. Would his love-making be as bold and over the top as his other habits?

She swallowed with a gulp, almost choking on a ketchup blob as a thought darted through her head. She spoke even as the quiver of intuition took hold deep in her belly. "Sex," she blurted.

He stopped pacing and stared at her, a strange but intense expression on his face, a French fry protruding from between his lips like a half-smoked cigarette. "Now?"

She shook her head impatiently. "Not you and me. The story. Maybe that's the answer to your question. Sex!"

He stared at her as if she'd completely lost her mind.

"It's the oldest story in the world." She rose. Now it was her turn to pace as she tried to make sense of the idea. "Mr. Cadman's having an affair, he's passing on secrets via pillow talk, he's putting investments in her name, he's—"

"Her, who?"

She just stared at him. How could he call himself a reporter and be this dense? "Someone who's looking awfully young and pleased with herself these days. Someone who's been out of town at the same time as Cadman. Someone who's in a perfect position to chatter to Harrison *Peabody* about things that are supposed to be top secret."

"No." He shoved another fry into his mouth and started pacing again. "Not Margaret Peabody."

"Yes. Margaret Peabody. You called her a hottie."

He swallowed and kept pacing. "You think Cadman and Margaret Peabody are jumping each other's bones. What are you basing this on? What facts do you have, what sources?"

She'd reached a wall, and turned to pace back to the computer. "Yuck!" she cried as she stepped on something warm and smushy. She raised a foot and pried off a squished French fry, then hopped to the bathroom to wash ketchup from between her toes.

"Intuition," she yelled over the sound of running tap water. "Gut level intuition." She waited for him to scoff at her "woman's intuition" but he didn't.

"Why?" he challenged.

How could she explain something she only just realized she suspected? She came back into the room, scooped another fry and chewed without tasting.

"He's been acting odd. He had his teeth fixed. His hair's been getting darker, not grayer. He smiles more."

"That's because he had his teeth fixed. He wants to get his money's worth from the new caps."

"It's not just that. We've both noticed he's been out of town a lot...and so has Margaret Peabody. At the same time. Maybe it's nothing to do with business but with love." She halted and they gaped at each other. Ty Cadman in love?

"But—"

"It would be interesting to see if her shopping trip and her spa vacation coincided with any of Mr. Cadman's business trips. Maybe she and Mr. Cadman *are* in love."

He blew air through his lips in a silent whistle, finished the fries then turned back to her. He tossed the empty box at her trash without even looking and it landed dead center.

"So what? Even if they're having an affair, how does it connect to Macarthur?"

"Let's suppose he's putting land in her name so people like reporters won't figure out what he's up to. It can't be coincidence that Margaret Peabody just bought land recommended by Mr. Cadman right around the time you see him playing golf with Nate Macarthur."

"Okay, Tess. Write it up."

"But—"

"I know, we don't have any facts. Write it up and see how it feels. Figure out what we need to know, what we've got to confirm. It's worth a shot."

A bubble of excitement bounced in her belly. "You think so?"

He tweaked her hair, a teasing gleam in his remarkable eyes. "I think you might one day turn out to be a real reporter."

She swelled with pride at the grudging compliment. "You really think so?"

He shrugged. "Hang with me long enough, something's bound to rub off."

Now came the fun part. Composing the story, piecing it together as best they could.

"Poor Margaret," Tess lamented. "Do we have to mention her in this article."

"If your hunch is right, we'll show the story to Cadman and if he loves Margaret, he won't let it go to press. He'll tell us everything."

"You'd blackmail Cadman?"

He shrugged. "All's fair..."

"And if I'm wrong?"

"You ever worked the obit desk? That could be the next assignment. For both of us. At some remote outpost in northern Alaska."

The tapping of keys was the only sound as she started to put together what they knew and what they suspected, weaving it with the hunches. Behind her stood Mike, leaning over her chair to watch the words appear on her computer screen.

She paused as she contemplated how much of this was pure guesswork. "This stays here, right?" She tipped her head back to look at Mike. "The last thing I need is a libel suit from a family friend."

"I don't need one, either. All we have to do is prove it's true."

Still her fingers hovered over the keys. "Until then, we do nothing. Agreed?"

"Yeah, yeah. Keep writing."

Feeling the keen excitement in her stomach, she went back to typing the story.

"You're using too many adjectives. Forget the flowery, stick to the facts." His hands settled on her shoulders and she felt his warmth and the soft wafting air currents against her hair as he breathed in and out.

"No. Don't refer to Margaret Peabody as Cadman's companion, it sounds like they're bridge partners or something."

"What do you suggest?"

"I don't know. Mistress?"

"Isn't that kind of like calling her a kept woman?"

"What do men usually call the women they're making love with?"

He paused deliberately, and she felt the heat behind her intensify.

"I, um..."

"Concubine?"

"'Concubine,'" she echoed as a flutter of lust danced along her nerves. "Sounds a little old-fashioned."

His fingers moved lightly over her shoulders and just touched the bare skin of her neck. "How about 'sweetheart'?" His voice dropped lower and turned husky.

Her fingers froze on the keys as she felt his touch burn into her flesh. "Sweetheart makes me think of beach movies from the fifties."

He leaned forward and whispered into her ear, "Lover."

Her stiff fingers moved, trying to type the word, while the breath caught in her throat. It came out *lober*. She giggled nervously then deleted and tried again.

The word hung there on the screen in black and white.

Lover

The cursor winked at her. There was utter stillness in the room but for her racing pulse and trembling heart and the soft, slow caress of his fingertips across her neck. She hadn't managed to shake her foolish crush on Mike Grundel. If anything, it had intensified as she'd come to know him better, until, it seemed to her, they'd arrived inevitably at this moment. Would they move forward to intimacy or back off?

She pushed another button and a question mark appeared.

Lover?

Mike's arm reached over her shoulder, brushing her hair so it whispered across her cheek. He hit the backspace key and she watched the screen, her heart pounding as he changed the punctuation.

Lover!

He stood next to her, lifted the hair off her neck and kissed her lightly on the nape. "Yes. Lover. I think that's a good word. Don't you?" His voice was as intimate as a caress; its effect as he whispered in her ear *was* a caress.

She licked dry lips, while his mouth moved to the side of her neck and continued kissing her. She let her eyelids drift shut, acknowledging how much she wanted this. "Yes," she said at last. "*Lover* is a very good word."

"I want you..."

"Yes..." she whispered.

"...to be my lover."

"Oh, yes." His lips nibbling her neck sent erotic messages darting through her body. It had been so long, and she'd denied her attraction for him with such determination, but now the wall of the dam was cracking. Crumbling, really, under a torrent of lust.

"Just for tonight." His words were still soft, but she heard the warning in them.

"Mmm." Tonight was a very, very long time. And at this moment she really didn't care if the world ended in the morning, as long as he kept going where he so obviously intended to take her.

Of their own volition, her hands rose to do what they'd longed to since she'd first seen him. She touched his black hair and found it silky-smooth but also strong and wiry. "You have such sexy hair," she told him.

His eyes gleamed down at her, predatory and hungry. "Did you save that file?"

"What file?" The words came out dreamy and slow in the stillness that surrounded them. This couldn't be happening. It shouldn't be happening. But it was. And her world felt suddenly, delightfully mellow-toned and honey-flavored.

With a soft chuckle, he reached across her and pushed buttons until the screen faded to black and the quiet hum of the computer fell silent.

Her nervous swallow was audible in the stillness. She was certain that if he listened closely enough he'd hear her blood had started to flow like tree sap warming after a thaw. Thick, languid and as rich as maple syrup.

His lips hadn't touched more than her neck, yet every inch of her skin tingled in pleasurable expectation. All her nerve endings had centered there, obsessed with the promise of the soft, velvety caress of his lips. Moving slowly, he made a leisurely trip to her earlobe and took it into his mouth, pearl stud and all.

"You're so warm." He sounded surprised.

Warm? He thought she was warm? She was so hot she must be personally contributing to global warming.

She couldn't move, or even think, and she was glad. Just experiencing this was enough. He'd been very clear that this was a one-off, so she didn't have to deliberate on what a man like Mike Grundel could do to her life. He had no intentions of getting in the way of her career or her plans. He'd do nothing but give her one night she had a feeling she'd remember forever.

One night.

She hoped he didn't have any plans to sleep—not even for a minute.

Slow and easy, as though he had all the time in the world, he trailed his lips up her throat, over her chin, and at last, at long last, came in kissing range.

Her lips pulsed in anticipation. That fast-talking, often cynically twisted mouth taunted her with its nearness. His face was shadowed, but the glint of his eyes blazed at her like those of a beast of prey staring out from the blackness of the jungle. And like the startled victim, she felt herself transfixed by the fire of those eyes. Helpless to move.

Unlike her jungle counterpart, she craved the attack.

Whatever he saw in her face made him pause and gently lift a hand to her face. He traced a finger down her cheek, as soft as a feather. "Last chance to say no."

"No!" she gasped in panic. "I mean yes. Don't stop now. Please."

The lips hovered nearer. "Only for tonight."

"Yes," she murmured. "Only for tonight."

He kissed her. His lips caressed hers, moving back and forth so softly it was a teasing torment. It was hard to believe this was Mike—brash, cocky Mike— kissing her with such careful finesse.

Then her lips quirked against his in amusement. Of course it was Mike. He tasted like ketchup. She reached up to still his head and encountered his thick hair. She ran her fingers through the amazingly silky strands. He hadn't seemed like a man with any softness in him, so it was a surprise to feel the satiny texture slip through her fingers and fall forward to tickle her cheeks.

Leaning over her, he braced his hands on the back of her chair, imprisoning her. She threw her head back in invitation.

In the dimness, he was a contrast in light and dark. The black hair and darkly glittering eyes, the white denim shirt open at the neck to reveal a hint of coarser dark hair... Then the whole image blurred as he kissed her again, this time with all the firmness she could wish for. His lips captured hers and forced them to his will, molding and shaping them with the ease with which he molded and shaped words and sentences.

She could barely breathe for the anticipation that was beginning to simmer inside her deepest, most secret places. It's just a kiss, she thought dimly. She might die of pleasure before morning.

As though he'd read her thoughts, he upped the excitement level a notch as his masterful lips opened hers and the wet heat of his tongue invaded her mouth.

Never had Tess used her lips and tongue and teeth for such effortless communication. Here, where they spoke without words, the dialogue was perfect.

couldn't resist. One was a challenge. The other had turned out to be Tess Elliot.

He gazed at the packing in progress and had to sit on the bed, his knees were shaking so badly. He'd almost left. He'd almost run away from the woman he'd been looking for all his life.

He glanced at his watch, calculated deadlines, and started typing.

16

Have you ever felt a longing so fierce, it lives inside you like a howling wind, or a crying child? That's how…

TESS FELT. Her hands halted above her keyboard, then she lifted her right hand to wipe a tear. That's how she felt, not how the character in last night's dismal movie felt. All the elation she'd experienced at yesterday's meeting had dissipated. She'd rewritten Mike's story and sent it to his editor, certain that would get him his job back. But she'd heard nothing. Obviously he didn't want his job back. Or her.

She'd lost her best friend and her lover and…and…

She rose and ran to the bathroom for a tissue. Darn it, the box was empty. She'd plucked it dry of tissues just as she had the one in her bedroom and the extra box she kept in the linen closet. She grabbed a wad of toilet paper and blew her sore nose.

Mike hadn't been there last night. It was the first movie she'd seen in months without him by her side. The *Star* had sent a stringer—a snotty freelancer with a degree in film who clearly saw himself as the next Spielberg—not even a real reporter to take Mike's place. As if anyone could.

She sniffed. Mike was going to hate California.

Maybe he was already there.

She sniffed again. Her review was about as exciting as the damp Kleenex crumpled on her desk. She'd have to work on her article at the office this morning. Not that it mattered.

It was time, as Mike Grundel had so eloquently put it, to move on. She dressed with care and applied extra makeup to hide the puffy eyes and red nose. If she was going to go, she'd go in style.

So, she wore a defiantly perky bright yellow dress and held her head high when she entered the *Standard* newsroom.

"Hey, great story, Tess," Steve from sports said.

She smiled at him. Everyone knew Steve wasn't the brightest bulb. Had he just got around to reading her story about Jennifer Cadman's engagement party? "Thank you, Steve," she said, polite as always.

"Good work, hot stuff!" someone else called.

Jonathon Kushner wandered past her desk and shook his head at her. "You and Mikey, huh? I knew he'd fallen for you big-time, but I never would have believed this."

Feeling more and more dazed, she reached her desk and grabbed a copy of today's *Standard*. The banner headline across the top read, "Eagles Win Over Casino" by Tess Elliot and Mike Grundel.

A strange sound escaped her. A combination moan, sigh, gasp and hiccup. She'd written the story for Mike, why had he thrown her gift back in her face? She scanned the first couple of paragraphs and her eyes bugged. This wasn't the story she'd written. And if she hadn't written this, then that meant...

"Hey, Tess. Earl wants to see you."

"Later," she said. The managing editor would have

to wait. Her heart hammered with hope as she grabbed her bag and fled.

Within ten minutes she was at the *Star* offices, racing up the stairs, hope and dread warring in her chest. She burst into the newsroom and then stopped, hope crashing. Mike's desk was clean, stripped bare of everything but a phone and a computer. It was as clean as a blank page, an empty apartment, a barren love life.

She took a step back, turning the way she'd come, hoping the tears would hold off until she got to her car, when a familiar voice stopped her.

"Hey, princess. Come see my new office."

She turned, hardly believing it was him. But it was. Mike, larger than life and twice as cocky, grabbed her hand and pulled her into a small office in one corner of the newsroom. News Editor, it said on the door.

"You didn't leave?" she said stupidly.

"Couldn't," he replied. It was hard to see through the film of her own tears, but his eyes didn't look quite dry, either. He pulled her to him and she threw her arms around his neck, kissing him for all she was worth.

A ragged cheer went up from the newsroom, and she blushed and giggled, trying to pull away. Mike kept her hand in his. "Staying here was the scariest thing I've ever done." He dragged in a breath. "But I'm about to do something scarier." He touched her face with his palm and gazed into her eyes. "I love you, Tess."

She needed to hold him, and he sure looked as though he needed holding, so she threw her arms around him. "I thought I'd never..."

"I never thought I'd say them." He hugged her

tighter, and whispered right into her ear. "There's more. I want to marry you."

She pulled back just enough to see his face clearly. "You do?"

"Yeah. That way my name will always come first on double bylines."

She chuckled shakil. "No it won't. I'm keeping my own name after we get married."

"Are you going to write our wedding up in the society page?"

She stopped and stared at him. He stared back. Then he began to laugh, building to a full belly laugh. "Mike Grundel on the damn society page."

"With his wife, Tess Elliot."

"Now look, I don't mind about you keeping your own name, but let's be reasonable. Why should our double byline always be in alphabetical order?"

"It won't," she assured him. "It will be ladies first."

* * * * *

Nancy Warren returns to Pasqualie, Washington, with two brand-new Duets stories!

A Hickey for Harriet

Hot sports reporter Steve Ackerman has his pick of women. When he finds out geeky co-worker Harriet MacPherson's lifelong dream is to be a cheerleader, he's determined to help her achieve her goal. Little does he know that underneath the twinsets and tweed hides a sexy pom-pom-wielding goddess!

A Cradle for Caroline

Former model Caroline Kushner has the perfect life—a gorgeous husband, money and an amazing marriage. At least, she did have a great marriage. She and Jonathon aren't exactly speaking right now, but not because her husband hasn't tried everything from covert meetings to kidnapping! He's determined to get Caro back in his life…especially when she finds out she's expecting the unexpected!

On sale April 2003

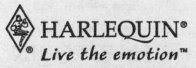

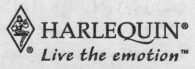

Hoffmann

Jacqueline
Diamond

Jill
Shalvis

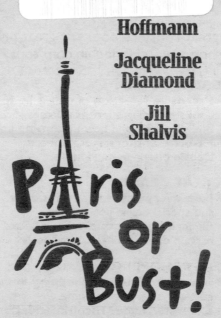

Paris or Bust!

A hilarious and romantic trio of new stories!

With a trip to Paris at stake, these women are
determined to win! But the laughs are many as three of
them discover that being finalists isn't the most
excitement they'll ever have.... Falling in love is!

Available in April 2003.

HARLEQUIN®
Makes any time special ®